Lealtad

Lealtad

Jorge San Martin Zambrano

AUTHOR'S NOTE

This book is a firstfruits offering to the Eternal, who gave me the mandate to write. Thus, I respectfully place my novel *Lealtad* and all my work as a writer at His feet because I belong to Him.

Prologue

I **TAPPED ON MY** new neighbor's side door, and right away, her silhouette loomed behind the frosted glass before the door swung open. Days earlier, she'd waved and smiled as she exited her car. Still, I'd avoided introducing myself, feeling unprepared to talk to a woman because the incident at work had shattered my confidence.

"Hi, Andrew," she said with a smile.

"How do you know my name?" I blurted and then cursed my clumsiness.

"Your mail was delivered here the other day," she said with a chuckle. "I've seen you walking your dog. I'm Felicia Smart." She held out her hand, and I shook it. "You live across the street."

"Yes, I do. I was wondering—"

"I'd love to take care of your dog."

I blinked in surprise. "How did you know?"

"You are not carrying a casserole dish, so I assume you're not welcoming me to the neighborhood. Besides," Felicia said, pointing at my hand, "you're holding a key."

"You're a step ahead of me. I've meant to come over, but to be quite honest, my life has been in turmoil, and it's true, we haven't talked before, but I need a dog sitter. School and work demand time, and he needs the company. Besides, you seem very nice, and I know where you live—I'd be indebted to you."

She tucked her long dark hair behind her ear and frowned. "I'm sorry to hear that. Would you like to come in?"

"I'd love to, but I have a meeting with my professor about a story I'm writing, and I'm late."

Her eyes revealed surprise, but there was no time to explain.

"Here's the key to the house and my phone number," I said, handing both over. "Whenever my car isn't there and you feel like taking him for a walk—it'll be good. His name is Hercules."

She eyed me. "Do you always give women a key to your house when you first meet them?"

I could feel my mouth open. My cheeks burned.

Felicia gave me a stern look and then laughed. "I'm kidding. I'll take good care of your dog. And when you have time, I'd love to hear about what you're writing."

"Sure," I said, trying to sound nonchalant, but I pictured her reading the real thoughts I wanted to describe on that page, and I swallowed hard. I even sweated a little. "And thank you so much for agreeing to look after Hercules. How much will you charge me?"

"Oh, come on. We're neighbors. Bring me a cup of coffee once a week, and I'll consider it settled."

We locked eyes. Felicia's were of the purest kind of blue. I forced myself not to stare and quickly said goodbye. Something prompted me to turn around before crossing the street. She was still there. I gave her my biggest smile as I got into my car. I couldn't remember the last time I gave a woman such a smile.

I drove to the university in twenty minutes flat, my best time ever, but I was still late for my appointment with Professor Levine. As I sprinted up the stairs, I tripped on the last step and fell to my hands and knees. The marble floors of the old building that housed the Department of English were uneven and cracked, especially on the stairs.

"Good evening, Andrew," Professor Levine said, looking at his watch as I practically tumbled into his office. "Let's see what you have for me."

The professor leaned back in his chair while I brushed myself off, spreading tiny smudges of blood over my clothes. The jagged marble had pricked my palms. Without missing a beat, he handed me his hankie. Flustered, I removed the manuscript from my satchel and began reading my first project of the semester.

Andrew Joseph is my real name, but that doesn't matter because everybody in the cleaning crew at the candle factory knows me by my sobriquet. At least, that's what Perico had hinted. "Is that the only fancy word you know, man?" I'd asked him, as he swept some dirt into his dustpan.

"You're not the only one with a dictionary, you know," he'd replied.

The nickname described my internal battle between malicious concoctions against my attacker, Jack Bennett, with his ugly scar below the glass eye, and my better side, the forgiving one—the yoyoing one.

"Oh, Better Side, you're almost dormant."

Professor Levine raised his hand.

I cleared my throat and twisted the ends of my long hair. I already suspected what he'd say. After all, this was my second semester with him. I'd become familiar with his mannerisms. He always asked me to read my stories aloud so he could hear how they flowed and get a feel for the rhythm and pacing. And when the story was spot-on, he'd make a circular motion with his right hand.

But ever since the assault, my work hadn't been up to his standards.

"Don't let your writing become stiff, Mr. Joseph," he'd said the last time I was in his office, with its Irish cream walls and light filtering through windows covered by leafy branches. The room where he whispered finicky words, such as *structure* and *flair*. Words that turned me into a boiling teakettle of frustration for many reasons.

Nevertheless, the professor's suggestions brought sense to my troubled stories. Before meeting Professor Levine, I associated the word *structure* with two-by-fours at a construction site, and when I thought about *flair*, I saw a woman dressed in fancy clothes and a white scarf that fluttered in the breeze.

Professor Levine looked pained behind his rimless glasses. His right hand remained still. "Kind of bland, don't you think? Action is golden, Mr. Joseph. You can do better." He gave me a thoughtful look and asked, "Why did you give the main character your name?"

Embarrassed, I scanned the floor-to-ceiling bookshelves, which were filled with the luminaries of British and American literature, except for some frisky South American writers on the bottom shelf. His laptop was the only sign of modernity in the room. Noting the garbage can beside his desk, filled to the top, I tamped down the urge to empty it.

"Nothing wrong with making yourself a character, but let me ask you this," he said, rubbing his semibald head, which was scattered with dark moles of all sizes. "Why? Writers are always in their stories, of course, but usually from a distance. You're right in the pudding." He interlocked his fingers over his chest and leaned back, closing his eyes. "Why do you want to be so close to the action?"

He was old. Maybe I could wait it out, not answer at all, and hope that the passing of time would make him forget his question.

I knew he wouldn't, though. Despite his frail appearance, he exuded power and commanded respect. And his tenor voice resonated with elegance, so much so that even his rebukes sounded like oboes playing arpeggios.

Interminable moments passed. Professor Levine raised one of his bushy eyebrows before fixing me with his gaze again. "Mr. Joseph?" He searched every inch of my face. "It's unusual for a writer to play himself. It creates many challenges. Do you think you have the chops for it?"

"No, but there's nothing worse than a coward."

From outside his office came the creaking of a chair. I knew whoever was on that chair had listened to our exchange. After all, many times, I'd sat there and taken note of the trembling voices while telling myself I wouldn't be like that, would be confident and brave—all while trying to stop my foot from tapping.

He nodded without adding a word.

"I might kick the bucket sooner rather than later," I said, shoving my hands into my dirty blue work fatigues and staring at my scuffed steel-toe boots. "I must be with the other characters to write this story properly. No distance. If I fail, I fail."

"Beg your pardon?"

I kept my gaze down.

"I want to save somebody's life before I say sayonara. He's a person drunk with his power. My boss." I dared a glance at the professor. "By the way, I might not finish the class because of this wrinkle."

His focus was steadfast. "You mean . . . literally?"

I nodded. "Yes. But I don't know, Professor."

The professor stood and turned toward the window, which offered a view, half covered by a tree with voluptuous limbs, of the Charles River. "You've taken me by surprise," he said, rubbing his temples. "I don't know what to say." Then he turned back to me and looked straight into my soul. "Elaborate on the saving part, please."

"Well, the story hasn't finished playing out in real time, and I want to inspire my boss to change his ways. Everyone has some good in them, after all," I said with a shrug. "If he doesn't change, there could be violent consequences."

The student sitting outside broke the silence with his cough.

Professor Levine seemed unfazed. "I see. In that case, you'll need to write an alternate ending. Right?"

I frowned. "Alternate ending? Why?"

"Because if you haven't finished saving this person in 'real time' when . . . well, when the angel holding a scythe says, 'Surprise!' . . . Sorry for my blunt approach, Mr. Joseph. But that's why I say write the alternate ending."

"That seems too advanced for me, Professor."

"Humor me," he said, narrowing an eye. "There's no such thing as advanced or beginner in my class. There are only writers. And don't push me, or I'll say three endings. Besides, didn't you just tell me there's nothing worse than a coward? Balls—metaphorically speaking, of course—that's what you need to write a riveting story."

I almost laughed as I imagined the face of the student outside the office.

"That's all there is to it," Professor Levine continued. His expression shifted, and he became the warm scholar who appeared at the most unexpected times. "Take chances if your characters aren't as alive as you want them to be," he said. "You keep taking chances. Edit and rewrite. But, Andrew, with flair, please."

My mouth twitched. "I've never written two endings for the same story, Professor." Writing one end sounded complex enough. Two? I wiped the sweat from my brow.

"Then learn the skill. Listen," he said, clearing his throat. "If you're gonna 'kick the bucket,' as you said so delicately, you might as well do it with flair on the page."

With that, he waved his hands like a symphony conductor, pointed at the clock, and gestured me out. I turned to leave. "By the way," he said. I glanced back. "What was the sobriquet?"

"Finish the first chapter, and you'll find out," I said while grabbing the bloody hankie, and hurried out. "I'll return it all clean." The pain in my eye was flaring up again. It felt like a needle pricking my eye.

I almost crashed into the student waiting outside his office. He looked terrified.

"Remember," the professor called from his doorway as I hurried down the steps. "I determine your grade. Bring me something I can read all the way through."

Outside, I dropped to my knees and screamed since the pain was so intense. After a moment, I regained my composure. The professor's comments were welcome despite their toughness. But the task ahead of me seemed daunting.

How was I supposed to write an alternate ending to this situation? It was out of my hands. It all depended on Bennett's decision. Or perhaps on Perico's murderous inclinations—and mine. My pen had nothing to do with it.

I went across the street to the convenience store to buy a chocolate-dipped vanilla ice cream bar. Then, I went to the roof where we went with Perico, and after I finished my treat, I tossed the stick, imagining it was Bennett twirling down and crashing on the sidewalk. I stepped back from the ledge, terrorized and in ecstasy at my sick thought.

I flew down Jamaicaway on my way home.

My wirehaired dachshund greeted me at the front door of my two-bedroom apartment in a two-family town house. The moment I stepped inside, my phone rang. I removed the device from my pocket and glanced at the screen. *Mom.* I sighed. Lately, she'd been wanting to discuss the most uncomfortable topics at the most inconvenient times. I placed the hankie in cold water before washing it.

"Hi."

"Hi, Andrew."

"I just got home from class a minute ago," I said, cradling the phone against my face with my shoulder. Walking into the kitchen, I noticed two wrapped chocolates on the counter and a yellow sticky note on the fridge:

Thank you for trusting me with Hercules.

I smiled. I'd never seen his name written with such elegance.

"Professor Levine and I discussed my story," I continued, hoping to steer my mom's attention toward something less contentious than usual.

She huffed. "A class with a demanding professor, on top of work—with those animals, no less. You must be exhausted."

"I am," I said. "But he's an excellent professor, and you don't have to be so tough on the guys. Perico's my buddy, and Chuchoka . . . Well, maybe you're right. He's a little wild."

"You should be out dating, son."

So much for diverting her attention—Mom was always predictable until she wasn't. I had no interest in dating, though. After my sister, Jenny, left us, I retreated into a shell. At first, I kept count of how many years had passed and noted every anniversary of her death. I'd stopped counting. What was the point? The recent attack had only made things worse.

Mom giggled and kept going. "I remember how much attention you used to get back when you still lived at home. You hated going to the store so much that you took your sister, but even that didn't help. Women kept coming on to you."

I looked at Hercules's inquisitive eyes and shook my head, as if he could hear Mom's nonsense. Though younger, Jenny had tried to protect me from all the opportunities for lust that lay bare before me.

I sighed. "Mom. Please. I can't deal with this right now."

"I'm saying this to cheer you up, Andrew. Go out more. Don't spend all your time writing. And who writes a story about a candle factory?"

I regretted having spilled my ideas for the first chapter to her. Professor Levine's advice rang in my head: *Your first draft is sacred. Don't spill it to the wolves.*

I bent to give Hercules his predinner bone. "The attention from women is nice, Mom, but sometimes I wish Dad hadn't endowed me with his good looks."

"Don't say that," she snapped. "You shouldn't feel sorry for being attractive."

"Well, sometimes it creates awkward moments, Mom," I said. "More than I can tell you."

Hercules whined for a treat. I shook my head, but he put his dark paws on my knees, scratching twice to make his point. "You once said, 'Don't do something only because you have the power to do it. Do it because it's the right thing to do.'"

"Well, you certainly know how to put a smile on a mother's face."

She paused. I knew there was more coming. "Is there something else going on with you? Something besides the robbery?"

"No, Mom," I said. "Just the robbery." I'd told her some guy had knocked me out from behind and taken a few dollars from my wallet while I walked home from Mattapan Square. She had no problem believing that tale since a while back, I'd been robbed at gunpoint by some teenagers. This was before I bought my car.

"That's not a small thing, Andrew." She hesitated. "That was all?"

"Yep."

"Where did it happen? Where, Andrew?" she said. "It had to be in that crappy neighborhood where you live. One robbery is one thing. Two is a sign to move out, baby."

"It's not crappy, Mom. Some decent people live here." *Felicia from across the street, for example*, I thought.

She sighed. "I don't know why you haven't moved back here with me. I'm all alone."

I braced myself for the oncoming guilt trip, which I didn't deserve because we both knew we needed to live separately. But she needed to say it to assuage her remorse for pushing me away. It happened every so often and had started to sound like a sticky melody.

"It would be an easy commute to work and school," she continued. "And here, you'd only have to contend with bears or deer and the occasional skunk." She laughed and then choked back a sob. "I never told you to move away."

"Mom. I'd rather not talk about any of this right now. I'm exhausted. Can you understand?" Sensing my words had stung Mom, I softened a little. "Listen, I had to move away. You know that. I needed distance. And you did, too, Mom."

She sniffled. "All I'm saying is that you've experienced so much pain, and you're still standing. I know you can overcome this, like the other time. Did the guy take more than cash? Anything of value?"

Nothing tangible, I thought.

"I have to go, Mom."

"Last week," she blurted, desperate to keep me on the line, "when I heard you talking about the villain in your story—what's the name?"

"Bennett," I said, as evenly as I could, "Jack Bennett."

"Right. The malice you described demands a setting with more stature. Andrew, you work at a university. Why don't you make that the setting for your story?"

I had to admit she might be onto something there. "I'll consider it."

"Universities are corporations, baby."

"What are you talking about?"

"You might think I'm naïve, but I know that learning isn't the only thing that goes on within those walls. It'll be perfect. Nothing happens at a candle factory."

"I'd wanted to avoid using my job as a setting, but the more you talk about it . . . it makes sense. Little job, little evil. Bigger job, bigger evil. I really have to go now, Mom."

I hung up, trying to untangle the emotions this knotty conversation had created from the ones the discussion with Professor Levine had stirred.

I walked in circles for several minutes, going from the kitchen to the living room while Hercules trailed my every step. Of course, the story would feel more authentic in the setting Mom had suggested.

But the prospect of so much reality on the page made me nauseous.

I threw a chicken breast into the iron pan and turned on the gas. The meat sizzled and soon smelled enticing. But by the time it was ready, I wasn't hungry, so I cut the whole breast into small pieces and put them into Hercules's bowl. Forcing myself to stop putting it off, I went down the short hallway to my office, which also happened to be my bedroom.

I opened my laptop and looked at the file. Then I dragged it into a folder labeled *Crappy First Chapters*. Professor Levine was right. The opening was "kind of bland." I needed a new one.

"Connect with the reader from the get-go," Professor Levine always said.

I scribbled a scene on my pad of yellow paper. I could see it clearly in my mind. "Yes, I've got it," I said to Hercules, who'd already wolfed down the chicken and pushed the bowl throughout the kitchen, something he always did once he'd cleaned the bowl.

My new first chapter would have plenty of action.

Chapter 1

Sunday, September 22

THE SPIDER DANGLED FROM an invisible thread above the steering wheel. The audacity. My jaw tightened as the blood rushed to my face. I raised an open hand, ready to punish the creature, but at the last second, I sighed and gently blew the thin-legged rascal out of the way.

Revving the engine, I inhaled the burning rubber. The car backfired twice. *Pow, pow!* And then I floored it onto Gladeside Avenue through dense white smoke.

Rain pummeled the windshield. Thankfully, it was only a five-minute drive to Perico's place, in Mattapan's rougher section. The wipers stopped working right before I parked outside the complex of gray brick buildings.

Jumping out of my car, I screamed his name in frustration. Water droplets cascaded down my face into the cigarette-butt-littered mulch beneath my feet. It was pure desperation. I'd lost Perico's address and knew only that he lived in this complex.

"Yoyo!" a raspy voice yelled back.

I peered into the dark to see Perico waving from a fourth-floor window. Half his hairy torso stuck out, illuminated by languid lamplight.

Disbelief shot through me. I hadn't expected Perico to answer. Truthfully, part of me hadn't wanted to find the apartment. Part of me had been attempting to fool my conscience so I could say I'd done everything possible to prevent the deed.

I knew he had a gun. He kept it in his bedside drawer. The .38 with the "mahogany handle," as he often told me. One day at work, I'd teased him so fiercely about the handle that he spat, "Ah, you know nothing. When did you last have a revolver in your delicate hands?" Then he'd scoffed. "Probably when you played with your yellow water pistol in the backyard, just before Mami came out to wipe your nose."

That had been two weeks ago. We'd been on the dark rubber roof of the university, where we always had lunch. We were on the same cleaning crew, and it was the same day he'd given me the nickname. "You're like a yo-yo that goes up and down on a string."

And so I became Yoyo for my buddies at work.

Then Perico's face contorted into an expression of agony. "What would you do if he'd done that to your son? Would you be so forgiving then, Reverend Yoyo?"

"Hmm," I'd said, taking a bite of my ham sandwich. "That's better than always being wrong."

Under the blazing sun, I lifted my middle finger while Perico mimicked playing with a yo-yo. It irritated the hell out of me. Still, I had to admit my attitude toward Mr. Bennett swung by the minute.

Now, I ran through the main entrance and up the dimly lit stairwell to the wide-open door on the fourth floor, soaked and breathless.

"What happened?" I said, panting. "The line went dead."

"Nothing," he said with a smirk.

I gulped. Perico's eyes. Boy, they were cold and cunning.

"I hung up," he continued. "I had nothing else to say."

He stepped backward, gesturing me in. He seemed to be favoring his right leg.

"Idiot," I said, entering what he called the living room.

He nodded his agreement as he tossed me a towel. I'd started drying myself off when the pain shot through my eye. My knees buckled slightly, and I held the towel over my face.

"Are you okay?" he asked, sounding confused.

"Yep. Never better."

This was the last place I wanted to be. "Murderpan." That's what Perico called this part of town.

But I'd put my fear aside because of what he'd said on the phone: "Tomorrow, I'm gonna double tap JB at work. He's gone. It'll be his birthday present."

"Perico," I'd yelled as the line went dead.

"I'm going to use your bathroom," I said, needing a minute to compose myself.

He pointed to his left, and I hurried in and shut the door behind me. I pulled the string above the sink so hard that it broke. The bulb sputtered but stayed lit. I took a deep breath and looked in the mirror. I always parted my hair down the middle, just like my dad had. When I was little, I loved watching him get ready for work, dressing in his best suit. Mom would glow as he kissed her goodbye.

"You got your mother's emerald eyes, deep and melancholic," my dad used to say. Those were the last memories I had of Dad; Mom never wanted to elaborate other than saying he went to work in a far land. And when I kept asking, Mom gave me her best frown. Jenny and I just looked at each other, went up to our bedrooms, and slammed the doors in unison.

"You alive in there?" Perico said from outside the door. His voice sounded as if it came from under the ground. His fist pounded the thin wood.

"Yeah, I'll be out in a sec." I touched my icy face as if feeling my cheeks and nose for the first time. My fingertips slowly moved to the spot at the back of my head. It was still tender to the touch.

I finished drying off, exhaled, and made my way to the dimly lit living room, where Perico lay sprawled on a tattered blue couch pocked with cigarette burns. Seeing me, he stood up and removed six bullets with pretty lead tips from his pocket. Then he grabbed my hand and slammed the creatures into my palm. They felt cold and heavy. So I put them back on the coffee table.

"I can get you front-row seats if you want to see him piss his leg. After what he did to you . . . Kiss the bullets, Yoyo. I want to see his eyes when I put the muzzle in his mouth. Let him suck the cold metal."

I swallowed and sat heavily on the couch. "What's this thing you have about the eyes?"

"You can tell if someone's afraid to leave this world or not by the look in their eyes," Perico said, smiling. "Sometimes they beg. Or cry." His grin disappeared in a flash. "I've never sought no one's approval for this type of shit." He glanced away. "But you gotta be on board, man." He looked at me again, his eyes wide. "This pain—you've made it mine, too. And it makes me feel desperate. I want to grab that fucker by the neck. See his eyes bulge."

Part of me took perverse pleasure in the image—Bennett's execution up close and personal. But as I gazed at Perico, I knew there was an abyss between us. "Look," I said. "I knew Bennett would never forgive me for defending Mrs. Mejia at the hearing."

Perico opened his mouth.

"But it was the right thing to do," I said, trying to defuse the conversation.

"And you still want to save him? After that fucker worked her so hard she lost her baby?" Perico said with a high pitch, while shaking his head.

After the hearing in court, things had gotten worse for me at work. The extra assignments, the constant pressure, the insults. The assault in the basement. Now, I had to stand up for myself. Stand up to Perico, to my mother, and, above all, to Bennett—and I had decided that the best way to do this was to write a story about it all and get Bennett to read it. One of the wildest concoctions of my life. To pull it off, I'd need a miracle.

The way I saw it, a bullet was too simple—almost an injustice to the innocent projectile. Bennett's crime against me was as personal as things got. His action demanded something equally personal, guttural even. The difference with my method of response to him was that I would inseminate his mind. And for that to happen, I had to get my hands dirty and busy on the page.

"So, you want my blessing, Perico?" I said. "No, man. I mean, I want to, but no. No!" I looked at my feet. "Murder isn't my bag, my man," I muttered.

"That's not the point, Yoyo."

I made fists and placed them over my eyes. "It's precisely the point." My voice broke. "Every night, when the demons sit at the foot of my bed and whisper in their malevolent voices—demanding blood—I feel like it's an option, but I battle them."

"Nobody understands your mumbling, you idiot," Perico said. "A bullet—everybody turns their heads. The next morning, you'll feel better. I guarantee it." He patted me on the back.

"I never asked you to make this pain yours," I said. "Offing him? That's a long leap."

Perico threw up his hands in exasperation. "You, of all people, should be fine with this."

"I might talk a big game and brew awful desires in my heart, but I'm battling them."

For a moment, Perico seemed entrenched in his thoughts. Then he laughed and stated, as if he hadn't heard a word I'd said, "I'm worried about the splash."

"What do you mean?"

"It might be challenging to hide it." He whistled while making a diving motion with his hand, starting from above his head. Then he clapped his palms together. Hard. "Pow."

My mouth dropped open, and I drew back.

"Yes. His body hitting the sidewalk will be a statement to the bosses and make them think twice about their cruelty." He grabbed the roll of electrical tape on the coffee table, held it up, and explained that he'd wrap a soda bottle around the barrel. "It'll function as a silencer if you choose the most discreet option."

"Oh, I have options with this, huh? You're messed up, Perico," I said. "You want him to take a dive for being cruel? Oh, man."

After they'd banished me to Jack Bennett's area, Bennett had targeted me immediately. During my first week under his management, about a year before the attack, he'd told my coworker Chuchoka, "There's something about Andrew I don't like. I don't know what it is."

I had laughed when Chuchoka told me. He'd never find out. Even if I told Bennett the reason right to his face, he wouldn't understand. He wasn't exactly a spiritual person.

Bennett supervised all aspects of the cleaning crew, so it was impossible not to be under his constant scrutiny. The director, Mr. Diedra, gave Bennett great latitude when it came to managing the workers.

"It's called retribution," Perico said. "Some people call it karma." He stared at me with a smirk. "Hey, he had his pleasure. Now it's time to collect the cash like whores do. But since we're not ladies of the night, we'll collect in blood." He cocked his head to the left. "Fair, isn't it?"

"Yeah?" I said, aware that my hands trembled. "And what retribution do I get after our deed is done?"

"I'll put a couple in him for you, baby. I've been thinking about this ever since Bennett told me. But part of me wants him to hear the thunder. Fuck the silencer."

He yelped, covered his eyes, and moved into a fetal position on the floor. Then, holding the .38, he pounded the floor as if it were Bennett's skull.

He looked deranged.

I ran to the bathroom and threw up. I retched until I was drained.

When I returned, I said, "I think you've gone too far." But I grabbed the bullets again and moved them so close to my mouth that my breath steamed them. I knew that if I kissed them, Bennett was done. But my ears did not believe my mouth as it spoke. "What can I do to change your mind?"

Instead of responding, Perico got a beer from the fridge, sauntered back to the couch, and started telling me a story from his days as a heroin addict. I'd heard this one too many times.

"The needle was stuck to my arm," he said, tapping his forearm, "and the dude put his hands in my pocket. My gun was in the back of my pants."

"So, what did you do?" I said. I already knew the answer. He'd never outright confessed to killing the man, but his body language and smug expression told me all I needed to know. Every time he retold the tale, I felt a chill. My best pal, a killer, sat next to me.

"What I had to," he said. He took a long sip and belched. Then he turned toward me and gave me a broad smile, revealing his discolored teeth. But there was sorrow in his eyes. Suddenly, he scrubbed his face with both hands as if something had splashed on it.

"Give me a nod or a look, and I'll run the errand."

Perico was unpredictable. One day, a week before the attack, I'd borrowed his buffer without letting him know. When I returned it to the storage room at the end of our shift, he was there, leaning on a stack of boxed paper towels. He avoided my eyes.

Afterward, I went to my car to find it keyed from the rear bumper to the front light. I hadn't seen him doing it, but I didn't need a map. He strolled out to the parking lot, giving me a wave and a two-dollar grin.

Driving home, I felt stupid to call such a man my friend. Perico's friendship reminded me of riding a roller coaster.

Still, he was my buddy. With him, I felt free to express the petrifying feelings I kept from everyone else.

As opposite as we were, we bonded over the intense strain of working for Bennett. Perico felt the pressure, too. Yet, around Bennett, he was the epitome of good servitude, bowing his bald head whenever he saw our boss in the hallway. But Jack Bennett didn't know how to take him, this submissive attitude that defied anger, encapsulated with a polite smile and a grin. Bennett often scratched his head after Perico performed this act. I'd told Perico, and his reply had been, "Yeah, but I know how to take him—by his bony neck." He'd lifted his hand as if squeezing something. His arm shook, and the veins in his forehead and neck bulged. I sensed Jack Bennett understood what Perico was capable of.

A few weeks ago, near the end of the summer, we'd been on the roof, which offered a view of the Charles River. A chilly breeze created a brownish foam on the waves, which disappeared as fast as they formed. A man on a megaphone barked orders to rowers. Our shirts flapped like flags. Perico stood on the roof's ledge, defying the wind to push him over the edge. Sitting had been dangerous enough for me; to stand would have been borderline suicidal.

Our exchange that day had been testy.

"What are you doing?" I said. "Do you want to die?"

"You can't take anybody's life if you're unwilling to risk yours."

"That makes no sense, you idiot."

He stepped down and faced me. "To you, it doesn't."

"I know that you'd prefer I hated the guy," I said.

How I saw it, when we raged about Mr. Bennett on the dark rubber roof, we were sorting out our feelings. It was like a workshop for our vile inner desires, but Perico didn't see it that way.

Now, as we stared at each other over the wooden crate impersonating a coffee table, I once again felt the weight of the revolting memory. I sank back farther into the couch.

In July, two months ago, Jack Bennett had summoned me to the mechanical room in the basement. *Come right away*, he'd texted. *Emergency.*

"I never told you what Bennett said to me," Perico said, once again reading my mind. "'I poked your friend Andrew. I thought you should know. And if you open your mouth, nobody will believe you. You're an ex-con. I got your actual record, not the bull you put down in your job application.'"

A sob burst out of me. I wanted to purge my insides whenever I relived what had happened after Bennett knocked me unconscious. Often, I'd get in the shower and wash until my skin became soft like a sponge.

I cleared my throat. "Con or not, couldn't we talk to Diedra? Tell him the truth?"

I knew we couldn't. But still, I had to say it.

"I don't understand you, Yoyo. Listen, when I was taking out the trash the other day, Bennett came up to me and said, 'I want you to say you saw Andrew take some supplies home.'"

Perico's eyes blazed with anger. "I told him, 'You got the wrong person, Mr. Bennett. The rats are in the dumpster.'"

"Just like that?" I asked.

"Yeah, just like that. And I knew the price of not betraying you would be steep. He's been giving me extra assignments, calling me a piece of shit every chance he gets. But I'm your friend. That's why I'm so fucking upset with you. You don't know the difference between your friends and enemies."

He punched his palm. "Bennett thinks he can get me fired, and then you'll be all alone."

I hung my head, feeling as if a heavy weight had leveled a blow to my gut. Bennett consistently tried to discredit me so that no one would believe me if I spoke out about the attack. Bennett's request to Perico meant that my assumptions were correct. And now he was making my friend's life harder, too.

"And you tell me to give that prick a chance," Perico continued. "I'll give him a chance, all right. I'll give him a chance to jump off the roof straight into the deepest part of hell. He'll fit right in. No problem, baby. *Best Manager.* That'll be the tag on his office's door in hell."

I met his gaze to find his eyes filled with tears. In all the time I'd known him, I'd never seen Perico cry—and his repertoire of horrible acts was extensive.

"Life was simpler before I met you," he said. Then he whispered, "Somebody tried to do that to me as a teenager. I took my time with him. Four days. Four long days." He didn't sound proud.

Of course, I was foolish for wanting to save his life. But there was something redeemable in everyone, wasn't there? And deep in my heart, I felt that the burden of Bennett's death would be worse than the one I'd been wrestling with ever since he summoned me into that basement.

Perico walked toward the window, then faced me in the part of the room where the bulb's electric light appeared tired. He looked like a menacing ghost, his face moving in and out of shadows as cars with bright headlights drove by the building.

"I vomited, man," Perico said. "When Bennett told me what he did to you. He told me on the fucking roof. Our place." Without warning, he swung around and punched the wall. He appeared not to notice the enormous hole he created.

"He just wants us to feel desperate," I said, shaking my head.

"He thinks nobody can touch him."

"But murder? C'mon, man."

I looked at the bullets. They lured me to smooch them.

Perico sat down next to me again. His eyes were barren, glassy. "He's gotta fly from the roof. Either he jumps off or I put two in him—one in the crotch and one in his face. In that order. I don't care if I go back to jail. I'll never see my baby again anyway."

Before I could ask him who this "baby" was, he snatched the bullets from my hand, loaded the weapon, and struck the cylinder with his left hand.

The rattling had hypnotic elegance. The mechanical sound of the cylinder finding its chamber soothed my ears like a drug traveling through my veins. But the words that emerged from my mouth contradicted my feelings.

"It's not that simple," I said. "You can't go popping people because they wronged you. Don't you understand that I'm trying to heal from this? I have to forgive him." I let my head fall back and stared at the cracked ceiling. "If I don't, the guilt will trap me for eternity."

Do you want me to end up like you? I almost asked. But I bit my tongue. I didn't want to hurt him. He didn't deserve that.

I gasped as Perico lifted me off the couch, shook me by the shoulders with his colossal hands, and threw me back onto the sofa with all his might. I landed with an enormous thump. He got up close to my face. The whole scene brought to memory his time as a bouncer. The stories had been wild and riveting when we sat on the roof, seeing the boats pass. But this time, I was the story.

"Forgive him?" he screamed. "Either you're out of your mind or not telling me the full story."

Moments later, there was a knock on the door. "Is everything okay there?" asked a timid voice.

Perico threw a heavy ashtray at the door. "Get lost!"

I heard a woman screaming in the hallway, and a moment later, a door slammed.

"It's the only way," I pleaded, despite feeling rattled. It wasn't the first time Perico had gotten violent with me. "Otherwise, you'll be a prisoner of your crime and make me one, too. Perico, man. When I wake up, I get on my knees and pray for the strength to forgive Bennett."

"Pray? Pray? Somebody does that to you, and you pray? Somebody does that to me, and they die. What kind of man are you?"

Perico lurched away and started pacing. The rain pounded the roof, and for a few minutes, I felt nothing. It was the first time since the attack that I'd felt any pleasure.

He stopped by the window again, and his mouth moved as if it were playing with a toothpick. "Okay," he said without looking at me, "but I'll strangle him on the spot if he ever mentions it again. No second chances. Doesn't matter if there's a hundred people around me."

I nodded and exhaled. I had negotiated a deal to save Bennett's life. But I felt filthy having advocated for him.

"He'll never change," Perico said, looking out the window, giving each word an enormous space. "I don't understand why you're so hell-bent on saving his life."

"Let me deal with this my way," I said, standing. "He did it to me, not to you." I walked to the door and turned back before leaving. "Look," I said, almost whispering, "Bennett has a daughter. Filomena. And guess what?"

"What?"

"One day, Bennett saw me with a book and said, 'Filomena loves to read. She's always giving me books.'" I looked down, away from Perico's scrutinizing eyes, feeling sheepish. "So, I'm going to write the story of what happened and give it to her, and then she'll give it to Bennett, and maybe he'll change. Of course, I'll alter his name and Filomena's. But I'm hoping that through the context, he'll realize how close he came to redecorating the sidewalk on his birthday."

Perico shook his head and made a dismissive hand gesture. "I feel better knowing I'm not the only crazy one in the room."

But then he limped toward me and embraced me with all his strength.

I mumbled a goodbye and staggered down the stairs toward the parking lot. Back in the car, soaked to the bone, I wept for a long time. Finally, I drove home and lay face down on the cold maple floor of my kitchen while Hercules licked the tears off my face.

The smell of ammonia drowned my nostrils as a fluid seeped through my shirt. I clutched Hercules to stop his violent shaking, and we both lay there in his urine's soothing warmth like two babies united in their mother's womb.

Chapter 2

PAGES FOR THE PROFESSOR

Monday, September 23

Gusts of wind had left Jamaicaway covered with wet leaves. It was as though I were driving through a tunnel while the yellow and brownish foliage streamed over the hood and windshield. The car skidded, leaving the tail inches away from hitting one of the trees that formed part of the majestic canopy.

The darkness hadn't dissipated when I arrived at the parking lot, and as I neared the building on foot, I covered my nostrils. The dumpster smelled putrid. With my other hand, I grabbed the one-gallon deodorizer next to the motor of the hydraulic pump that helped to compress the trash into the back of the chute. I poured the liquid inside and slammed the green metal door.

A few feet away from the green beast, Perico puffed on a cigarette as he did every morning. He trailed me to the relic of an elevator, and I heard him dragging one of his boots.

"The smell doesn't bother you?" I asked.

"What smell?" Perico said. I glanced back to give him an incredulous look and noticed his eyes were red. "Can you help me open my classrooms?"

Every Monday morning, we unlocked about seventy-five classrooms. We had to complete the task quickly before the students showed up for classes.

I slowed to let him catch up. "Sure, but what happened to you?"

"I drank too much last night after you left," he said, popping a couple of breath mints. "I can barely walk."

I nodded but remained unconvinced. I'd seen him with a hangover before, but something was different this morning. "We can ask Mrs. Mejia to help us. Let's keep it from Bennett." I dug into my pocket. "You need more mints, man," I said, handing him an unopened package.

"Mrs. Mejia already went down to the office. I didn't want to ask her. She's pregnant again, you know?"

I knew. Everybody knew. "Hopefully, she'll have better luck this time," I said. "I'll just ask her to do a few near the office. That way, she doesn't have to walk too much."

"What the hell does luck have to do with what happened to her the first time?" Perico asked and spat near my foot.

I let the question go unanswered. He was right, and I had no desire to get into a discussion about it.

When we entered the narrow cage, my stomach lurched. Bennett was fixing his red tie by the brassy control panel. Surprising as it was, it acted as a perfect mirror for him.

"Gentlemen," he said as the doors closed.

We nodded our greetings.

Subtly, Perico lifted his eyebrow, pursed his lips, and pulled an imaginary trigger behind Bennett's head with temerity. He got the hand behind his head so close that it was impossible for Bennett to see the fingers mimicking a trigger.

"Happy birthday, Mr. Bennett," Perico said while glancing at me. His deep voice rumbled in the suffocating cage.

"Thank you, Perico," Bennett said without turning back. "Thank you for remembering."

"I had a gift for you at home. It's wrapped in blue velvet. But my buddy Andrew said it wasn't appropriate for someone of your stature. Told me the mahogany was fake. I'll get you something better."

"No need to worry. Your thought is what counts."

I gave Perico a hard stare. From the corner of my eye, I could see Bennett continue to preen and admire his reflection. Unbidden, a memory of a Monday morning from a while back that I wanted to forget surfaced, creating a stir in my stomach.

I'd ridden the elevator with Mrs. Mejia, who was on our floor-care team, one morning. "I call this place the Shrine," she said in her caramel voice. "This is where Bennett worships his reflection in the brass."

"Worships himself?"

"Yeah, scrawny boy loves scrawny boy," she'd said. Then she repeated the joke to the crew in the office. Everyone had burst into raucous laughter. She hadn't known Bennett had overheard.

The faint light of the Shrine this morning made Mr. Bennett's eyes resemble hollow caverns in the brass. Catching my eye, he smiled. I took an involuntary step back. And then, before the doors opened, Mr. Bennett slid his hands down the brass. My stomach turned. I knew what was about to happen.

I followed him into his pocket-size, bare-walled office, where the crew awaited marching orders.

"Any volunteers to shine the elevator this morning?" Mr. Bennett asked. It was a rhetorical question. He knew his pick.

She'd made another joke at his expense yesterday while he was talking about his background as a sailor. "A sailor?" she'd said to us, once again loud enough for him to hear. "A sailor? Maybe in his tub with a rubber ducky!"

Bennett scanned the small group and stopped on Mrs. Mejia. It wasn't a terrible assignment, but the chemicals eventually made us dizzy.

Bang!

Bennett slapped a fly on the desk, right over the sign-in sheet, smudging it with red. The crew called it the redundancy sheet—because we scanned our IDs on a card reader. It was Bennett's clumsy attempt to control the room's mood.

"Did I see you volunteer, Mrs. Mejia?" Bennett said. "Great. Please take a white rag and brass solution. You'll love how it looks when you're done."

"Remember, Mr. Bennett, I already lost one baby because of this crap. Two would be criminal on your part."

Mr. Bennett's face paled.

"Those are ugly words, even for you, Mrs. Mejia."

"There are no ugly words, only ugly hearts. Words are innocent workers, Señor Bennett."

"Our help just evaporated," I said to Perico as we left the office. "But I can manage most of them."

We parted ways, and as I walked through the hall's opening doors, I couldn't stop thinking about Mrs. Mejia. The day it all began. That day in his office, after the laughter had subsided, Mr. Bennett had informed her she'd be on elevator duty. "Don't worry about doing anything else this morning, Mrs. Mejia. Stay in 'the Shrine,'" he said, making air quotes, "until lunch today. In fact, it will be your task for the next two weeks, since you're so familiar with it."

Mrs. Mejia looked terrified. "But I'm pregnant and don't feel too good."

"Then go home and mark sick on the sign-in sheet," Mr. Bennett said with an innocent smile. But Mrs. Mejia had used all her sick and vacation days on doctor's appointments already, and Mr. Bennett knew it. So it was polish the elevator or take time off without pay.

A few hours later, I heard her vomiting in the bathroom near the office. Her yellow rubber gloves lay outside the door. The chemical had melted away the fingertips. When she emerged, she was sickly pale.

"I never said you couldn't take a break if you felt sick, Mrs. Mejia," Mr. Bennett said. "Right, Andrew?"

I said nothing, stunned, speechless at his cruelty.

Two weeks later, Perico and I found Mrs. Mejia sitting on the stairs leading to the basement, her head buried in her lap.

"It was a baby girl," she said.

About a week after the showdown in Perico's apartment, I saw Filomena on the couch in her father's office. I was finishing my shift. She placed books and a laptop with a decal of the university logo into a backpack. The orange laces on her white sneakers were the sole pop of color on the aseptic VCT flooring. Something about her put me at ease. Her angelic face? Or perhaps her curious eyes, which seemed to notice everything.

She spotted me and smiled. "I overheard some guys talking, and they say you're Yoyo now," she said, tilting her head to the side. "I like it. I heard it's because you don't let anybody put you in a box. Is that true?"

I chuckled. "I'm glad you see it that way. But it wasn't meant as a compliment. You're Mr. Bennett's daughter, right? My dog does the same thing—tilts his head sideways—when something strange comes out of my mouth."

She grinned. "Sorry, I'm Filomena," she said, extending her hand.

I moved forward to shake it.

"Don't worry about what they say."

"I don't."

How could she be Bennett's daughter?

"Are you a better person after reading whatever you read?" I asked her, nodding toward her bag.

"Nobody has ever asked me that question," she said, looking thoughtful and running her fingers through her golden hair.

"A while back, a professor posed the question to me. I didn't have an answer either."

"How about I think about it and then give you an answer?" she said. Her thoughtful look relaxed me.

"The best answers come that way."

"So, a professor said that to you? Are you going to school, Yoyo?"

"Yes, here. I've seen you around."

She looked surprised. "You should have said hi."

I shrugged. "I guess I feel strange navigating these two worlds."

"Why?" she asked with a frown.

"They're far apart. Here," I said, gesturing to the office and the hall beyond, "I'm in a stony dungeon."

"A dungeon with chains and a half-naked man wearing a dark leather mask?" she said, with a mischievous look on her face.

I laughed. "Close. But more screams and foul odors."

Her smile widened. "So, how do you cross the divide?"

"I change out of my blue-collar shirt and run with all my might, but there's a rope tied to my waist. It's long enough that I can cross the abyss but short enough that I always get yanked back."

Our gazes met in the lifeless office.

At that moment, Bennett walked in, rigid, arms crossed, glaring at his daughter. *We don't talk to the help*, his look said.

I pulled at my T-shirt, struggling to breathe as I quickly made my way to the door, not even bothering to sign out.

"Bye, Mr. Yoyo."

I turned. Then, under Bennett's intense scrutiny, I added, "Anyway, I'm nobody here. I buff floors. I appreciate the thought, though."

I tipped my imaginary cap in deference to him and headed out, but what was on my mind was defiance. I wanted to let myself hate every bone in his body. It would be easier that way.

Perico was close behind me the next day when I clocked in. Bennett approached, clenching his fists. "I don't want you talking to my daughter."

"It was nothing. Innocent talk. Do you know what that means?" The words left my mouth without asking me.

His eyes got small.

"So, what is this? Are you trying to follow in Mrs. Mejia's steps by playing with words?"

"Oh, no. Mrs. Mejia has had that talent from the womb."

Moments later, Perico and I headed to the storage room to get our buffers. "What's eating at that MF?" Perico asked as we attached new twenty-inch white pads to our buffing machines.

"His daughter talked to me yesterday."

"He doesn't want you talking to her, but he can assault you?" Perico said with a scoff.

My anger grew by the day. It was like watching my car's tachometer as I floored the gas pedal, running into the red, ready to burst.

In the elevator, I could feel Perico staring at me. "Are you okay, man?"

My emotions were visible now. Impossible to hide. I looked at the long hallway as the elevator door opened. "Let me make these floors beautiful today," I said, exiting the car.

"Yoyo," Perico said. "Be cool. Don't let him get to you. I'm here."

I whirled around. "Like you were in the basement that day?"

I regretted my words when they spilled out, but I needed a target.

"How could you?" Perico whispered.

I sighed. "Sorry, Perico," I said, and afterward, I went back and forth with the buffer for several hours, spraying wax on the tiles and watching the brightness overcome the dullness.

Perico was right. We needed to eliminate Bennett.

That night, I tossed and wondered, for the first time, whether things would be different if I were not in school. I wanted to finish. And speaking out about the attack could jeopardize that. I had seen people fired because of trumped-up charges. So, this time, I kept my mouth shut even though I wanted to scream with a megaphone from the rubber roof what the coward had done.

Mrs. Mejia hadn't kept quiet after the miscarriage and wanted justice, not hardcore vengeance. And I was the one she had come to for help. She'd cried in my living room about her loss, and I'd no heart to turn her down. But when I defended her in court, I knew the odds were against her. The best she'd get was a chance to sob for her baby in court—a mirage of justice for the poor.

I often wondered how my life might have been different if I hadn't taken up her cause. But that was more Yoyoing. The one thing Perico hated about me. He once told me, "Don't wonder why you got into a fight once the fists fly. It's a sign of weakness."

The giant man was right. I was in a fight now, and I wouldn't quit.

Chapter 3

Friday, October 4

THE ENTRYWAY TO PERICO'S building felt moody, and the narrow stairs creaked under my weight. The often-loud stereo in the third-floor apartment spewed silence. But it was the foul odor in Perico's place that truly spooked me.

In his one-room apartment, white curtains fluttered over a packed suitcase beside his bed. His breathing was heavy in the softly lit room, and his white T-shirt had vomit stains on it. He held a framed photo over his chest with a tight grip.

I was checking on him because he hadn't shown up for work since Monday, and my calls had been going to his voicemail.

His eyelids flickered. "I think I'll have to go to the hospital," he said, without surprise, as if he'd expected me to show up.

I frowned and tried to ignore my growing unease. "Anything serious?"

"The doctor said something about an infection in my leg—and on top of that, complications from my heart condition." Perico tapped his chest and shook his head. "He gave me some meds, but I'm not touching the stuff."

I clasped my fist and wanted to punch him for his stupidity. Instead, I asked, "Can I take a look at your foot?"

He nodded and covered his eyes as I lifted the blankets. For his sake, I did my best to contain my horror.

"I think you should take the gun," he said. "It's in the drawer."

I didn't move. The image of Perico's leg had frozen me to the spot.

"Take it," Perico said.

I dropped the blankets and exhaled. "You sure, man?"

"Yeah. I can take a bullet in a gunfight or a knife in a dark alley. But a nibble at my leg day after day? And this smell. The gun's a temptation."

Perico's eyes got moist. "This thing has been going for a good while. I didn't want you to know. Didn't want to put another burden on you." He sighed. "But at least dear Mr. Bennett will survive me, thanks to you. You've done some stupid things before, but this one . . . I had it all ready to go. It would have been beautiful."

He laughed so hard that he coughed blood into a towel beside the bed. That's when I noticed several whiskey bottles strewn on the floor.

I reached for the drawer and there it was, the revolver with the "mahogany handle," wrapped in a blue velvet bag. I grabbed it with my index finger and thumb.

He turned his head toward me. "It's not Hercules's turd, you idiot. Grab it like a man."

I glared. I didn't know how to hold this weapon with conviction, to let my hate flow into the trigger without remorse. Or doubts.

I also wasn't sure how I felt about introducing this explosive element to my house. It would be as much of a temptation for me as for Perico. But he'd suffered the consequences of our tumultuous association for months.

He'd always helped me, and to ask for anything went against his nature. I had to step up.

"Treat it with respect," Perico said, "for what it can do." His words sounded as if they'd come out of a meat grinder.

I nodded. Sadness threatened to overwhelm me, but this time I remained stoic for Perico.

He set the framed photo on the nightstand and stood with much effort. "That's my daughter, Bellatrix. She was almost eleven when I took this—right before I went to jail." His eyes moved as if they were traveling to another place, another time. "I hope she's okay. I haven't seen her since I was arrested." He shook his head. "One day, Chuchoka told me he thought he saw her at a store near my place but went quiet when I asked questions. I even shook him. Wouldn't say a damn word. Bastard."

"He can be tight lipped when he wants to," I said.

He looked at me with a glimmer in his eyes. "If something happens to me, you need to find Bellatrix. Promise? Ask Chuchoka to help you."

"Sure, man. You got it," I said. It was a sobering thought, to look for the lost daughter of a man who had done so much for me. It wasn't something I could just dismiss or forget. But more importantly, it brought home his possible death as something that was around the corner.

He hobbled out of the bedroom section and over to the kitchen area with a cane, unable to put much weight on his right foot, which I avoided looking at. The stove's electric coil became bright red in a flash, and he boiled water for coffee.

Perico seemed deep in thought, so I said nothing.

"So," he finally said, pouring us each a mug, "let me see if I got this right, my dear Yoyo. You're writing this tale of me wanting to off Bennett, hoping his good daughter reads him this concoction of yours?" He tapped the counter twice, then took a sip. "You're writing this so Bennett knows that you, of all people, saved his miserable life?"

There was a pile of dishes in the sink, and the counter hadn't been wiped for a while. I wrapped my hands around the mug, feeling the burning heat. "Why do you say Filomena's good? And it's not about Bennett knowing I saved him. I'm not saying I'm a saint, Perico. I don't want to be canonized. Do you follow me, private eye?" I sighed, frustrated. "Look, if you knew your life was about to end next week, wouldn't that impact how you lived this week?"

He frowned. "There you go with your philosophical crap again. What's your ideal outcome here?" He tapped the cane on the floor. "You're thinking he's going into the seminary? Perhaps he'll confess? Or do you want him to apologize? To say 'I'm sorry. I was bad, dear Andrew.' Is that what you want to hear?" This time, he smacked the floor hard with the cane. "I'm the one who drinks, but you're the one who acts like a drunkard with these romantic tales."

"So, you screw up once and there's no chance for redemption?" I said, with my annoyance building again. "So, we're doomed from the moment we mess up? Your life is simple, man. If someone screws up, you kill them. Make an error, condemned for life. That's a chilling universe, Your Grace."

The look on his face made me glad he couldn't move fast.

"Let me put it in terms you can understand," Perico said, without any anger in his voice. "I'm not proud of my awful actions, but I'll be truthful—I enjoyed most of them. It gave me pleasure to have the power to exact my own justice. And you, Yoyo, what does it say about you? I saw your face when we talked about killing him. You didn't feel just a little taste of satisfaction?"

"I'm not sure."

"You're not sure? C'mon, don't give me that shit. At least be honest. This is a world of actions and inclinations. Pretend all you want. But if I put you in a room with a whore, we'll see where you stand."

I swallowed and couldn't hide my shudder. I panted. But he was right. I enjoyed some of our machinations about Bennett. And if all that Perico said about me was true, what did it mean for the rest of my life? Exploring the good and the bad within me was petrifying and exhilarating at the same time.

"Do you think Bennett didn't enjoy raping you?" He leaned in close with difficulty. "That's where your answer is, my friend. The rest is bull. He enjoyed it."

I paced, perturbed to my core. "Then let me ask you this," I said. "Would you have helped me, cared about what happened to me, back when you were doing all this creepy shit you've told me about?"

He became somber. "Probably not, my friend. I don't know. I was just into myself, my pleasure." He lifted his hands. "Sometimes truths are colder than lies."

"So, you've changed," I said, nodding, satisfied that I'd made my point. "Don't you see it? People change, man. If you cut their life short, then you deprive them of that opportunity."

Silence fell between us, and he gave me a halfhearted smile, impossible to decipher.

"You asked why I called Filomena good," he said.

"Yeah."

"It's simple. She must be good, since she's the reason you'll let what happened to you happen to another person."

Perico's words came in rapid succession, and their force made me shiver.

"You didn't think you'd be the only one, did you?" he said, getting close again. "You're responsible for Bennett's next victim. Their blood will be on your hands." I felt his breath on my face.

"That's not fair, even for you." My eyes welled up with tears. "Why are you tormenting me?"

"You know, Yoyo, when something is rotten, you cut it off," he said, glancing at his foot. "Bennett has tasted the rush of doing something evil. And once something like that is in your body, it doesn't leave. So, what's my name going to be?"

"What's your name going to be?" I asked, confused by the sudden change of topic. But it was his habit to hold on to things I said, like phrases and words. Then he hit me back with them at the most unexpected moments.

"You won't use my real name, genius. Or do you want the police to pay me a visit?"

He had a point. But I liked his nickname. Perico.

"How did you get that wild moniker, anyway?"

"Moniker? Oh, aren't we fancy today? My old buddies and I nicknamed the humongous joints we smoked *pericos*. Something massive. Got it?"

A wild thought rushed into my mind. "I'll have a woman play your character."

"I always liked you because I thought you were secretly a lunatic," he said with a chuckle. "How is a woman going to kill somebody like Bennett?"

"It's not always about being an animal with brute force." I took a big sip of my lukewarm coffee. "I should get going, man. Do you need anything? A ride to the hospital?"

"I need to crash with you. My landlord is going to evict me."

I blinked. "Are you serious?" I said. "And how would Hercules feel about your company?"

Perico shrugged. "Weren't you the one talking about being good and all that hooptedoodle?"

"Hooptedoodle?"

"Yep, it's bullshit talk. Anyway, you can come get me in the morning. Gives you time to prepare and talk to Mr. Hercules about it. But take the suitcase today. Less to worry about tomorrow."

I scoffed. "Yes, sir. You got it all worked out, huh?"

With a sigh of resignation, I retrieved the suitcase from near the bed. On the nightstand was the framed photo Perico had been holding. I peered at it. A beautiful little girl with long hair and a mole on her left cheek.

"My baby," Perico said, coming into the room. "I hope she's okay, wherever she is. I miss her."

"Pretty name," I said. "It sounds strong."

"It should. It means *female warrior*."

I wanted to offer him some words of encouragement, but my head was in turmoil. "I'll pick you up tomorrow morning."

I quickly left the apartment, almost tripping on a wayward shoe by the door, and then barreled down the narrow staircase. I'd been trying to avoid the guilt of not saying something and allowing Bennett to mess up someone else's life. But it was impossible to dismiss the thought now.

Perico's words played on a loop in my head: *You're responsible for Bennett's next victim.*

Chapter 4

Saturday, October 5

THE FOLLOWING MORNING, I found Perico resting his wide frame against the window overlooking the parking lot, the one out of which he'd stuck his naked torso the first time I visited. His cane held the remaining weight. He didn't turn around when I came in.

He'd jammed the rest of his possessions into a supermarket bag. We didn't have to worry about moving furniture, as he'd rented a furnished apartment. And anyway, there wasn't much of it except for a large bed, the tattered couch, a kitchen table, and two raggedy chairs made of pine.

Near the window was Perico's rubber tree. "Could you?" he asked, pointing at it. Approaching, I sensed his nervousness. An almond-shaped green leaf glided to the floor. He looked pained at the sight. "My little girl loved rubber trees."

"I got it, I got it," I said, picking up the leaf and handing it to him.

He hobbled to the kitchen sink, wetted a paper towel, wrapped the leaf's stem, and put it in his coat pocket. Then he returned to the bedroom, grabbed the framed picture of his lost daughter, and put it in his other pocket.

Perico labored with every step, and I had to take the supermarket bag from him. I let him lean on my shoulder. On our way down the stairs, we passed an older woman. Her back kissed the wall, and her eyes glistened with fear.

"I'm sorry for knocking on your door that day," she said. "I didn't know if you were okay."

"Don't worry," Perico said. "I know I haven't been a good neighbor. But in my defense, my friend here irritates me sometimes, so I have to shake him a bit. You understand, right, Mrs. Vargas?"

She nodded with her mouth open and then sprinted up the steps.

"I'm sorry for my foul language, Mrs. Vargas!" Perico shouted to the fast-closing door.

The five-minute trip to my place passed in silence, but I often glanced at Perico to ensure he was okay. It was a straight drive on River Street to Gladeside Avenue until we took a sharp right—going up a slight hill.

"Sorry to inconvenience you, Yoyo."

I waved away his apology. In the last few hours, I'd come to peace with the fact that he'd be living at my place.

"You put yourself on the line for me. I owe you."

He was my friend. And anyway, I was sure it would be a brief stay. But perhaps this was a hopeful thought.

Hercules and I would be gracious hosts and also make sure he got the care he needed.

"No cigarette butts on the mulch?" Perico asked as I parked in my driveway.

I smirked, hoping his sarcasm was a good omen. "I'm sure you'll take care of that."

"Not to worry," he said, making a yo-yo-like motion with his hand. "I'll be on my best behavior. After all, this isn't Murderpan."

I scoffed.

We heard the barking before I opened the door. Inside, Perico leaned down to pet Hercules. My dachshund sniffed his foot with a connoisseur's intensity, entranced by the unfamiliar scent. Then he wagged his fluffy tail, signaling his approval of Perico's coming into our home and his favorite space—the living room. Suddenly, Hercules lifted his leg over Perico's and sprinkled it with a few drops.

My jaw dropped. He'd never done that before.

"Well, that's one way of saying 'Welcome home, buddy,'" Perico said, laughing it off. "He branded me."

"Hercules," I said, but he ignored me and went to check his food bowl.

Perico walked a few steps, supported by his cane, threw himself onto the right side of the couch, and was snoring minutes later. The giant cane slipped from his hand, and Hercules, who'd just entered the living room, spun to escape. He looked at Perico, then sat down at his feet, facing me, as if he were his new guard dog.

"It's okay," I said. "You can look after Perico."

With that, Hercules jumped onto the couch and curled up near Perico's hand. It was a sight, the colossal man next to my slim dachshund.

After letting him sleep for a while, I showed Perico to the guest room. The small room with yellow walls had plenty of light, suitable for his rubber tree, and it faced the fenced backyard. His head was only a couple of inches from the ceiling.

"You can sit there," I said, pointing to the armchair by the window, "and watch the bluebirds. It'll take your mind off any problem. After the attack . . ." I cleared my throat. "I spent hours in that chair. The nest is on that branch," I said, gesturing toward it. "Not far from the trunk."

Perico nodded his approval and rubbed my back. "You'll be fine when I'm gone. Do you believe me?"

My eyes welled up. Perico was doing it again, comforting me when it should have been the other way around. I didn't believe him, though. And I refused to let myself believe he'd be gone.

For dinner, I prepared a chicken stir-fry with white rice, which he devoured. As we ate, we remained quiet, which was unusual for us. As long as I'd known him, he'd never depended on somebody else. It was an unfamiliar experience for me as well. Jenny was the only other person I'd felt I had to protect.

And that hadn't ended well.

On Sunday, I tried to make him as comfortable as possible, offering blankets, pillows, and warm beverages. Hercules collaborated with me, sensing that companionship was Perico's most present need. He often stretched out against Perico's healthy foot while my friend napped.

I called the hospital, but getting his doctor on the line proved impossible. Finally, a nurse told me to take him to the emergency room if he got a fever.

On Monday morning, I headed to work as usual. Perico had insisted, and he seemed well enough to be on his own for a while. Before leaving, I went to Felicia's place. She answered her side door in a bathrobe.

"I'm so sorry for bothering you so early," I said, flushing slightly, "but a friend who's very sick is staying with me. Would it be too much to ask to check if he's doing okay?"

"Not a problem. I'll take Hercules out a little earlier than usual and check on your friend. If there's any trouble, I'll call you."

I exhaled. "You're a lifesaver. I'll throw in a full breakfast with that coffee I owe you."

"I'll remind you," she said with a chuckle. "Go to work. I'll take care of everything."

"I owe you."

"You do," she said, giving me a beautiful smile while waving me off. "Go, go to work."

"Yes, dear," I said, returning hers.

Once at work, I went straight to Bennett's office. "Perico is sick, and he's staying with me. I may have to leave early to take him to the hospital if he gets worse."

Bennett raised his eyebrows. "Tell him to call me. I haven't heard from him in days."

"He's barely conscious," I said, and began to leave before my rage became too evident.

"Just so you know, Perico left a cryptic, slurred message. I didn't understand it. His time off is unauthorized—I mean, he doesn't have any sick time or vacation—we're already short," he said, raising his voice.

Insensitive prick, I thought. "If he continues to deteriorate, I'll need some time off. I have four weeks of vacation time accrued."

Bennett exhaled in disapproval and then shrugged with palms up.

I hadn't been able to help revealing the extent of Perico's illness to Bennett. It was true that its seriousness would leave me further vulnerable in front of my attacker. But if he wanted to try anything, I had enough anger stored that now—

I stormed to the storage room to grab my buffer. Perico's was where he'd left it.

Two hours later, I returned to find Chuchoka there.

"Any news about the big man?" he asked.

It was shocking to hear a complete sentence from him. Most of the time, Chuchoka spoke in monosyllables and grunts. Even Bennett treated him with politeness. Perico told me that, when Bennett was curious about the reason for my nickname, Chuchoka said to him in our basement lunchroom, "Sometimes it's dangerous to know certain things." After that, he got out his switchblade and stabbed the orange with fury to the table. Bennett took two steps back, according to Perico, who had been there then.

"He's staying at my house. He's pretty sick, man, and I'm starting to worry."

"Tell him I hope he gets better," he said. "And if he needs me to run an errand for him, I can."

He gave me an indecipherable look and tapped my arm twice. His eyes shone like gleaming coals. I knew better than to ask. Chuchoka was more disturbing than Perico.

I promised Chuchoka I'd let him know any news.

My phone rang. It was Felicia.

"Come home right away," she said. "Your friend is unconscious on the living room floor, and his forehead is burning. I've called the ambulance." In the background, I could hear Hercules howling. He sounded like a siren.

My stomach dropped, and I thought that my worries were turning into reality. Who would protect me now? That was my selfish thought as I headed home.

Several days later, on my way to Perico's hospital room once again, I passed a tall woman dressed entirely in black leather and wearing sunglasses. She wasn't just stunning—something about her felt familiar. But she barely glanced at me.

Shortly after I entered the room, a junior nurse came in dressed in blue scrub bottoms and a top filled with cartoon characters.

I'd had a few beers before coming to the hospital. My shame was getting to me. I'd noticed Perico favoring his right leg for weeks. And I'd chosen to ignore it, too caught up in my situation.

The nurse put something in Perico's IV.

"He'll sleep for a while," she said.

"Did somebody just visit him?" I asked, wondering about the woman in black.

"Yes, but he was barely awake. Though this morning, he was alert and talked on the phone." He only talked to one other person besides me: Chuchoka.

When the nurse left, I settled on a small sofa beside the bed and began a borderline-delirious soliloquy. In the background, the beeping of the heart monitor provided a hypnotic rhythm.

"I thought you were going to leave me, my friend," I said while I held his hand, which was double the size of mine. "When Felicia told me she found you on the floor, I saw the next steps unraveling before me. It was a lovely funeral service. Fitting. In attendance were the preacher, Hercules, and yours truly. A few days ago, you said, 'After I'm gone, have Hercules pee on my coffin.' Remember?"

I stood and walked to the window. There was no motion in the tree branches outside. There appeared to be a cemetery across the street. My senses struggled to determine what was reality and what was hallucination. My panic increased with every beep on the monitor.

I went back to Perico's bed and stood at the foot of it to continue my conversation with my friend's supposed corpse.

"At your funeral, I wore my black suit with a white carnation on the lapel," I said, slurring my words a little. "The preacher waited for me, with his little Bible under his arm, next to the cheapest casket I'd ever seen. A single rose rested on it."

I coughed, trying to sober up.

"I suffered for you, my friend. Alone with only my dog. It felt right to have my rascal at the funeral, since he'd offered you such sincere affection in a short time."

There was a light tap on the door, so I pressed my lips together. The young nurse peered in and interrogated me with her eyes.

"I'm just talking to him," I said. "He's my best friend."

She raised an eyebrow. I realized that she could probably smell the alcohol on me.

"Keep it low so Mr. Sanchez can rest," she said.

I hadn't been aware of my volume. I returned to the small sofa and kept going, albeit more quietly, giving voice to my emotions and hallucinations.

The preacher gestured to Hercules. "Is this the friend you talked about on the phone?"

"Yes," I said. "I hope it's not a problem."

The preacher looked around. "Well, he won't bother anyone." He attempted a stiff smile.

It was a given that I'd let Hercules pee on the mountain of dirt next to your casket, but the preacher looked dumbfounded at Hercules's irreverence. To defuse the situation, I said, "The deceased's last wishes, Your Grace."

"In that case, carry on," he said, but he looked pissed.

And I know he was pissed because he tapped his leg twice. Something Mom used to do when she was annoyed with Dad.

The memory made me smile. In the hospital room, the lights were now off, making it harder to distinguish the real from the surreal.

The preacher composed himself in the face of my impertinence and asked, "Do you want to say words for your friend?"

Just then, a huge raven landed on your casket and started pecking at the rose next to the cross. It sang a cutting lament, and Hercules barked in response. You should have seen them. But I shushed Hercules when I noticed the preacher's face was redder than hell.

"Mr. Joseph?" the preacher asked, eyeing Hercules while his mouth contorted.

"Okay, Father. Here I go. And don't forget, you asked."

He nodded with pursed lips.

"Perico, my terrifying but loyal friend, I always wanted to give you a profound answer—to convince you that eliminating a person never solves the problem. I had to contemplate the atrocity inside me, and then I would leave it behind when the time was right. No bullets. A bullet pierces and destroys. But the mess inside the one firing the gun doesn't go anywhere. It rots. Like your leg did."

Hercules chased the raven, which now had the rose in its beak, to a nearby tree, where it taunted my canine.

The cleric looked to heaven. Yes, he did, and then he spoke between his teeth. "This eulogy is way off-script. Way off, Mr. Joseph."

I heard people running in the hallway.

"Code blue," a voice said.

I returned to the bed and kept going.

"How's healing going to arrive otherwise? I had to clean the wound spiritually. I mean, not me, but God." I looked at the preacher, hoping he'd agree with a sympathetic nod. I needed somebody to lean on. Instead, he gave me a look that suggested I didn't know what I was talking about.

I looked back at the casket, my face flushed with anger— I heard the monitor beeping like a metronome. Steady. Draconian. The only sign that life was still there within my friend.

"You complicated the whole thing, Perico. I know, I know. You thought you were making things right with your proposal to make Bennett fly. But you incited a war within me. Well, maybe that's not fair to you. The battle raged before you ever knew about Bennett's attack. My problem is that I don't know evil as you do. I'm not saying that there isn't malice in me. But the truth is, I don't understand Bennett. Maybe if I understood the reasons behind his behavior, it would be okay to let him fly. Don't you think, Reverend?"

I had other words to say, but they dried up in my mouth. They felt like sandpaper over my tongue. I burped. The smell of rancid beer floated into the room like a cloud.

Perico made a noise and grimaced slightly. The IV dripped steadily.

"I hate you, big man. All those muscles and you couldn't stay alive a little longer?"

The preacher gave me a look of reproach now. Yeah, the nerve of him, but I charged ahead, standing on a barren prairie with no trees to hide me except the one where the raven perched.

The soft tapping on the preacher's leg was constant.

"Who's going to protect me now? Well, you didn't save me the first time, either. But it feels different knowing you're not there to grab the asshole by the neck and toss him over the ledge if I need you to do it. You know?"

The preacher raised his hands and took a step back, clearly shocked by the flurry of hate.

"There was safety in holding that thought. I lulled myself to sleep some nights with the image of Bennett flying from the roof."

"Son," the preacher said, pointing at his watch.

I hung my head, with sobs caught in my throat. The preacher's eyes expressed bewilderment and rage.

"That's all, Father," I said. I pulled Hercules's leash, and my heart drummed in my chest. "Let's go, buddy. Let's get out of here."

"Do you want to confess, my son?" he said with a throaty voice, coughing a little.

"Confess, Father? You've got the wrong person."

The preacher only nodded with the look of a man who'd seen it all.

"Ask Perico to get up and confess. You'll have business there for a while, Father."

"Son, it's not good to harbor resentment."

"Your Grace, I loved the man but didn't agree with some of his actions." I caught myself and heard my words. I sounded sanctimonious. The raven seemed to agree. It began a frantic lament. Hercules barked. The preacher and I looked at each other in silence.

"I'll tell you what," the preacher finally said, looking at his watch again. "Come to the church and you and I can talk. You don't have to confess, but everything will be confidential."

"Aren't you listening to me?" I said, getting so loud that Hercules growled at the preacher. "I want to kill somebody, and I hate this corpse for leaving me alone, and you think I'm ready for confession?"

With that, he turned and walked away. I lost sight of him amid the grayish mausoleums, the beautiful green lawns, and the occasional bluebird perching on the cold granite.

In the car, Hercules sat in the passenger seat, and we drove around the city. Eventually, as if the car knew where to go, I arrived at your parking lot. But this time, the trip up the stairs led me nowhere.

There was no one to wrestle against. Now, it was all on me. I sat in your empty apartment there for a while. The tears refused my summons.

"There's a moratorium on tears until further notice," they said in their crystalline attire.

"I don't know if I did the right thing, stopping you, my friend."

Perico made a noise but looked peaceful in his bed. The morphine dripped into his vein. It was as if the elixir of hell were dripping into mine. I kissed his hand before saying goodbye for the night.

At the door, I turned around. "Before I forget, Chuchoka said he could run an errand for you. What did he mean?"

Nausea overcame me, and I ran to Perico's bathroom to throw up. When I exited, the nurse waited next to Perico's bed.

"You're disturbing him," she said.

I went home with an even heavier burden on my shoulders, feeling as though I hadn't done well by him. When I walked into the house, I found Hercules lying near his food bowl. Two small chocolates sat on the counter. They put a slight smile on my face.

The next day, before sunrise, my cell phone rang.

"I regret to inform you that Mr. Roy Sanchez died at two in the morning. Cardiac arrest." The silence that followed was interminable. "Are you there, Mr. Joseph?"

I dropped the phone on the kitchen floor, shattering the fragile glass.

Chapter 5

PAGES FOR THE PROFESSOR

Sunday, October 20

CHUCHOKA YELLED TO THE sky when the clump of dirt hit the cross. A gasp whooshed through the four attendees like an invisible incision. The intense pain made me labor for every breath while Hercules looked at me with his pure brown eyes.

As the torrential rain searched every crevice of my clothing, my friend's departure acquired a heavy reality. I crumbled to my knees while I had the distinct sensation that his spirit was no longer on any part of this earth's surface. There was no plane to catch, no ship to board, no road to traverse. He had ceased to exist as Perico, and if I ever saw him again, he'd be a different entity. His uniqueness was forever gone. All I had left of him was his gun, the little girl's picture, the rubber tree, and my memories. The gun wanted to thunder, the little girl I had to find, the rubber tree thirsted for water, and my memories lusted for Bennett's neck.

My surreal eulogy at the hospital was no match for this moment of reality.

I'd put Hercules in my satchel, and he'd been quiet for the most part. Near us stood a woman with dark glasses. The same woman I'd seen at the hospital. She looked as though she didn't want anybody to talk to her. I saw her fighting her emotions, trying to suppress tears. Her stiletto boots were splashed with mud and bore tiny smudges of green.

The preacher had to stop the service twice because of the thunderous rain. Nobody else spoke. It was fine that way. Words didn't have a chance, like in my private eulogy. I prayed for Perico, hoping that God would consider the thing he'd done for me so unique that the weight of his faults wouldn't tilt the balance against him.

When I returned home after the burial, the town house at Gladeside Avenue had a palpable emptiness. I'd felt it even before I got the call from the hospital, a sort of premonition. But more than anything, I missed his honesty, crude and unrefined.

That week, at work, I avoided speaking to Bennett.

Though Perico had stayed with me for only a few days, I kept hoping to hear the soft rumble of his voice. Hercules also moved around the rooms, looking for the big man. He whined in the bedroom with the yellow walls until I lifted him onto the bed. He wanted to see for himself.

I left Perico's things untouched, as if he were on a trip, and I waited for a postcard every day. But I moved the photo of his daughter from the nightstand in the guest room to the coffee table next to the brown couch, his lounging spot. Before setting it down, I peered at it. She looked tall for a ten-year-old, the girl in the white dress with a mole on her left cheek.

Shortly before I went to bed, Felicia called to offer her condolences. "I'm here if you ever want to talk." I thanked her and told her I'd take her up on her offer soon. Then I toured the house again, Hercules by my side.

My dog got up on the couch and pressed his moist nose against the cushion Perico had rested on. Then he looked at me.

"I know. I miss him, too."

That night, as I tried to sleep, I wondered how I'd ever be able to convey Bennett credibly as a character. It was going to take a lot more than changing the setting of the story.

———

The following day at work, I touched the wall next to the green dumpster to convince myself I wasn't hallucinating. I even did a 360. I needed time to mourn in private. At the end of my shift, I gathered my courage and marched into Bennett's office.

"Perico passed away. I want to take some of my vacation time."

"I know," Bennett said. "I got a cryptic call from Chuchoka alluding to that. When did he pass away?"

"Over the weekend. On the thirteenth."

"Yeah, that's right. Chuchoka said that. Normally, I require at least a week's notice for time off. But I'll make an exception. Is two weeks enough?"

It was the first hint of humanity I'd seen in him. It was promising. "November sixth sounds better. If I need more time, I'll let you know."

"Yes, fine. No problem," Bennett said. "I'll fill out the paperwork. I had to cover for Perico by requesting people from other areas," he said with a mixture of annoyance and victimhood.

I remembered something I'd said to Perico during one of our many arguments about our boss—nobody was good or bad all the time.

"How did he die?" Bennett asked.

"Cardiac arrest. He had a heart condition and advanced diabetes."

Bennett grabbed his chin as if in deep thought. "I told him to take it easy. 'Don't get worked up about anything, Perico,' I said."

There he was. The Bennett I knew, ready to rewrite history on the fly. His goodness had lasted less than a minute. But for a moment, he'd fooled me. For a moment he'd seemed genuine.

I looked at him. "Perico was stubborn. And loyal to the death, don't you think?"

Bennett narrowed an eye. I'd taken a jab, but he couldn't weaponize any of my words against me. He looked down at his paperwork. "Take care, Mr. Joseph. I'll see you on the sixth."

As I walked out of the office, Filomena approached. She looked as if she wanted to talk, but small talk felt out of reach, so I headed straight for my car after nodding a silent greeting. The river, a stone's throw away, flowed with majesty, but up close, the water appeared murky.

I thought about going to see Professor Levine. His office was nearby, and our chats always energized me.

I quickly decided against it. The conversation with the boss had zapped all my strength.

Chapter 6

Tuesday, November 5

"**THEY REDID THE FLOORS** a few days ago," Professor Levine said, pointing to the gleaming hardwood. Golden dust covered his bookshelves. "But the poly scent is a bit strong for me." As he finished talking, I placed the all-cleaned hankie on his desk. He nodded and smiled.

The professor's breathing appeared shallow. The smell stung my nostrils, and my lungs thirsted for fresh air. I could taste paraffin on my tongue.

"Do you have something for me?" he asked, opening the window wider.

"Yes, pages filled with action," I said, setting the manuscript on his dusty desk.

"Action, huh," he said with a skeptical smile. "I'll be the judge." The venetian blinds fluttered in the breeze. He coughed twice. "Would you mind if we went outside? Who knows what I'll tell you if I keep breathing this stuff."

"Not a problem, Professor," I said, as my head throbbed.

He grabbed the manuscript and the small leather bag that bore his initials and then headed down the stairs at a slow pace. I followed. Once outside, we made our way to a bench by the river. The tall reeds at its edge waved at us.

"It's my favorite spot," he said. "I come here before class when the weather allows it." The sunlight made his wrinkles more prominent. He caught me observing him and gave me a stern frown.

"Age will come for you, too, if you survive your ordeal, Mr. Joseph."

"It's not like that, Professor," I said, caressing my neck and feeling sheepish.

I'd been thinking about the passing of time. I saw him as an accomplished man who gracefully accepted the vulnerability of aging. Perico had fought his own feeling of helplessness with the belief that he had the power to take others' lives. Bennett seemed not to concern himself with vulnerability. In his arrogance, he displayed a sense of invincibility.

Professor Levine shook his head and began reading, removing the dreaded red pen from his white shirt pocket. I scribbled a line on the pad of yellow paper that I always carried in my satchel. *Unbridled power, how terrifying for you to exist without fetters.*

It was an unusually warm day for November.

For a few moments, I sat impatiently, waiting for the professor to ask me to read the manuscript aloud. He didn't.

Instead, he nodded after reading the first few pages. His fingernails scratched the paper occasionally, creating the only sound between us. And so I settled in and watched the golden reeds dance to soothe my nervousness. My shirt was already damp with sweat. So much rode on these pages.

Once he'd finished reading, he placed the document on the bench between us as if it were breakable and dabbed his forehead with a white hankie.

"I think we have something here," he said. "It needs polishing, of course, but it's a good rewrite."

He took two yogurts from his bag and handed me one along with a plastic spoon. I accepted his offer.

We ate in silence for a minute. Some students walked by, headphones on, with the weights of their worlds on their shoulders. Others lay sprawled on the grass near the benches. Their distant chatter sounded like crickets and faded into the background as our conversation intensified.

"I have an idea for the first ending," I said.

"Well, before we get into that," he said, taking another bite. "Will you tell me what's going on? Your 'kicking the bucket' comment is relevant to the story, so I need to know. As your professor."

I set down my opened yogurt. "No one else knows about my diagnosis, not even Mom. The specialist believes it might be cancer," I said, pointing to my right eye, still staring at the reeds. "But nothing's for sure. We'll wait and see if the doctor's initial diagnosis changes after some time elapses. I'm under observation at this point. And I don't know how to feel, Professor. If I'm to die soon, finishing the story is the only important thing." I swiped my hand across my forehead.

I glanced at Professor Levine. He wore a look I'd never seen before. Paternal, perhaps. "I want to finish the story sooner rather than later, Professor."

He nodded. "This may sound cold, but consider the alternate ending an insurance policy for the story. We'll get into that. I have another more pressing question, Andrew. Why haven't you explored Yoyo's reasons for not exposing Mr. Bennett? Because, well, what if Bennett hurts somebody else?" He looked up at the sky. "Level with me—this story is fiction all the way, right?"

I looked straight at him. He continued looking at the sky. "Fiction to the end, Professor."

His wrinkles deepened as he contained his laughter.

I stared back at the reeds, but my chest was still tight from my previous statement to the professor. "But I do grapple with the question daily as I draft this story. It's not a straightforward situation. Can someone really blame Yoyo if Bennett commits another evil act? If he feels guilty about not outing Bennett, surely that's the burden the protagonist must bear. But I agree with you. I have to explore the subject."

He nodded. "This eye thing. How sure is the specialist? Because to put it boldly, you need to make sure the story still reaches its intended audience, even if you die." He dropped his voice so low I could barely hear him. "I'm sorry to be indelicate. I'd never say this to another student. I mean, this is the rarest situation in all my years as a teacher."

I shrugged. "Nothing is definite at this point."

"That's tough." He stood and walked away a few steps, then turned around. I thought of Perico and the speech he delivered in his apartment advocating for Bennett's execution.

"You know why I never ask the groundskeepers to cut off the branches crowding my window?"

I squinted. "I can't say I do, Professor."

"Because every living thing deserves to keep living without mistreatment. That's what I believe. Our dear Mr. Bennett challenges that premise," he said, pointing at me. "But I'm not prepared to toss him over the roof."

I burst out laughing. The release of tension felt good.

He scratched his head. "What's crucial is to establish Yoyo's true motivation for saving Bennett's life. Is it tied to another issue in his life, perhaps?"

Nothing got by the professor. "I'm establishing that connection."

"Right. I'm not saying that it isn't enough to let someone live. But it feels like there's more to the story. And all the narrative strands have to meet at some point— Currently, all the main characters work at the same place. Do you see what I mean?"

"I see your point, Professor."

"Also, there has to be a change in Yoyo. Growth. Character development. Unless you're writing a tragedy. On the other hand, some writers feel it is okay if a character doesn't grow, even in a nontragic work. Yes, sometimes art captures a glimpse of life's aberrations. Do you understand what I'm trying to say?"

I shook my head.

He returned to the bench and sat down. "The beauty of a story is that each character can follow their own path. A writer doesn't necessarily have to adhere to conventions. Some might believe there needs to be character development, but that's only one way of looking at things. So, how do you look at life—at writing, Mr. Joseph?"

"I hear you."

"Right now, as far as the reader knows, Yoyo hasn't spoken up about Bennett's attack because it would jeopardize his chance of finishing school." He raised his shoulders. "And another thing. What's the source of Bennett's strength? Nobody acts so boldly in their cruelty unless somebody has their back. Does his boss have his back?"

I had to admit that his questions were excellent. I looked down at a patch of grassy dirt.

The professor sighed. "This is more than a simple story, Andrew. It has a reality flavor to it."

"Well, didn't you once tell us that life and fiction will always intertwine? Mostly, I'm trying to show that forgiveness is a process. It's not instantaneous. There are stages to it, like grief, and it takes place after an internal battle."

He meditated briefly. "Convince me on the page," he said, tapping the bench again.

"But what about the endings?" I said, unsettled by the turn this conversation had taken.

"What about them?"

"You haven't asked me about them, Professor," I said. "You told me they mattered, but you're not asking me about my ideas for them."

"Well, Bennett gets murdered in one of them. Right?"

I inhaled sharply. "It's too soon to say, but I have some ideas."

"And the second? It can't be straightforward. Consider his insatiable need to suppress others."

"The second ending will be unexpected. You can count on that."

"And who's this fellow, Chuchoka? He seems ferocious. A weasel. I sweated. You saw me."

"He's that and much more."

"Chuchoka, does the name mean something?"

"It's a steaming corn soup, heated outside over a wood fire. People in the lower class eat it down in South America. But whoever laughs at Chuchoka, well, they should write their will first. Bottom line, Professor, he's primal. An animal."

"What about all the nicknames?"

"It's how the characters in the cleaning department remain sane. They make caricatures of each other through their nicknames."

"I see," he said. "So, what's Chuchoka's real name?"

"Not John Smith, that's for sure."

It was the first time I'd ever heard Professor Levine laugh from his belly. A student walking by gave us a quizzical smile.

"Next time, bring me at least twenty more pages. Let's see where your inspiration takes you. You seem to be writing at a good clip."

"I recently took some time off, but I think I can keep the pace." Pain shot through me, and I put my hand over my eye. "Thank you for asking about my health," I said, glancing at him.

"I'm sorry you're hurting."

I acknowledged his words with a nod. At that moment, I realized what I cherished most about Professor Levine. He never lectured me. Never imposed. Instead, he constantly challenged me to look at my stories from different angles, sometimes even irreverent ones.

He stood to leave. "You might want to use Filomena a little more. But I'll leave it up to you." His eyes shone as he flipped an imaginary yo-yo, as Perico had often done.

I waved my index finger, letting him know he'd struck a direct hit.

"One more thing. Bellatrix might be crucial to the rest of the story now that Perico is gone, right?"

I nodded. "Bellatrix will likely play a significant role. We'll see. I was thinking she might be the continuation of Perico's murderous inclinations. I can't reveal everything at this stage, though, Professor Levine," I said with a wry smile. "You told me that action is golden, but I believe mystery is supreme."

He responded with a grin of his own.

A student flew by on his bicycle, missing us by inches. Cars rushed by on Storrow Drive. The river was peaceful but murkier than ever.

I thought of the morning that Jenny and I filled the blender and didn't put on the lid. Mom had walked in to find the white kitchen cabinets covered in blueberries and cream. That's what writing this story felt like.

Still, as I walked toward my car, I felt somewhat relieved. Turning on the blender that morning had resulted in chaos. But the moment had also been exciting. Jenny and I had dared each other to do it. We'd felt powerful.

There was power in sharing what I'd been keeping secret for so long—Bennett, the cancer, all of it.

Now, I had to dig deeper. I had to search for the reasons why Bennett was still alive. I had to dig into the still-raw wound that Jenny's death had created in me.

Driving home after my appointment with the professor, while I navigated the curvy Jamaicaway, over which trees formed a leafy canopy, my phone rang, startling me. I hit the brakes, made a sharp right turn, and parked next to a baseball field. A little boy practiced hitting a baseball under his father's watchful eye. They had the field to themselves.

It had been heavy in my mind—to start the healing process between my mom and me. Yet I needed to let her know what had happened in the basement at work. Another complication in our already knotty relationship. There was no good time or place to tell her.

I picked up the phone.

"How did your meeting go?" Mom asked. Sharing my schedule with her had been a mistake, but I did it after the attack at gunpoint to calm her down.

"It went well. Look, Mom, there's something I have to tell you. And please, don't ask me a flurry of questions."

The boy hit the baseball over his father's head, and they ran to each other and embraced.

"Sure, Andrew. Are you okay?"

"No questions for a moment, Mom." I took a deep breath. "You know the attack I told you about?"

"Yes."

"It wasn't a robbery. My boss assaulted me." There was silence on the line. "Are you there?"

She cleared her throat.

"He raped me," I said. My voice trembled despite my best efforts to keep it steady.

Mom sighed. Complete silence filled the line.

"He knocked me out. When I woke up, my pants were down, and he was standing over me, pulling up his zipper."

Mom whispered. "You should have never left the house after Jenny . . . passed away." This time, she sounded sincere.

I hadn't wanted to, at least not so soon. But right after Jenny died, Mom withdrew from everything, including me. We passed each other in the hallway and kitchen without exchanging words.

"Mom," I said. "Whenever you saw me"—my voice cracked— "you saw the accident. You were so angry with me. I could see it in your eyes."

"Let's deal with the now," she said. "What can I do to help you?"

There she was, calm and collected. Where was the chaotic sobbing that Jenny's death had elicited? The fury? Her tone suggested we were sharing apple pie recipes.

"Nothing, I just needed you to listen," I blurted, fighting the urge to hang up. "This is something I have to do on my own. The story I'm writing helps me little by little."

"May I read it?"

I scoffed. "Some scenes might be too brutal for your taste."

"I want to, son. Give me a copy when you finish it." She exhaled. "This is certainly more than I thought I'd be dealing with today. I have questions but won't ask them right now." She paused. "Maybe you can visit me soon. Will you think about it?"

I felt a rush of gratitude. She did care. She was just trying, in her own way, to do what was best for me. "I will, Mom. I think I need to visit you."

I pressed on in a conciliatory tone.

"And I needed to tell you what happened, so you'd understand why I've been so moody lately." I ventured a little further. "We also need to talk about . . . the accident. When I visit."

"You know how I feel about that subject," she said, her voice suddenly hard.

"I need to forgive my boss. It's the only way I can heal and move forward." I took a shaky breath. "And I also need you to forgive me. It was an accident, Mom. There was a blizzard." Tears welled up in my eyes.

"Don't you think this is too much in one day?" she snapped.

"I can't hold the pain inside anymore, Mom. I've waited years for you to be ready. You know, if I hadn't left, this thing at work never would have happened."

The words came out in a rush, and I regretted them as soon as they'd left my mouth.

"Oh, so I'm responsible for what happened to you there?"

I slumped back against the seat. "No," I muttered. "That's not what I'm saying. Jenny's death has weighed on me for years. I need to heal, and for that to happen, I need you to forgive me."

"It should weigh on you. Do you think you can just wipe out Jenny's death and live guilt-free?" She let out a wail. "She's dead. And you're alive."

I shivered. Her words had cut me to the core.

"Mom," I said, interrupting her frantic crying. "Mom, I didn't mean to upset you."

"Yes, you did. Okay, since it seems you've been waiting for this moment, let's talk about it."

"Take it easy."

I heard glass shattering. My heart rate picked up. Still, fighting was better than not talking at all.

"Tell me how Jenny died!" she screamed. "Spare me no details."

"Are you sure?" I'd never shared the details before. She hadn't wanted to hear them. All she knew was that she'd died on impact against a tree because of the snow.

And so I did. I told her the storm had been raging and that visibility was low on our way back from Jenny's boyfriend's house. The boy Mom hated because of the stories she'd heard about changing girlfriends every month. I didn't tell her how fast I'd been going. Too fast for the conditions. I told her how the vapor rose from the engine after the windshield shattered and Jenny's blood trickled down her face. But I avoided telling her about the ditch where her lifeless body rested, out of the explosion's reach.

Mom cried for a long time. Then, she said, "Come home, my son."

I contemplated the field. The boy missed the ball often, but his father kept encouraging him. "You can do it." Each time, the boy's face brightened. I stayed there until it got dark.

Chapter 7

PAGES FOR THE PROFESSOR

Wednesday, November 6

FIRST, I GRABBED MY small knife and put it in my pocket. Then I went to Perico's old bedroom and opened the nightstand. There it was, wrapped in the blue velvet bag, formal yet ready for service. I pressed the side of the weapon against my cheek and took a deep breath. My knees became weak with desire. A few minutes ago, I'd been resolute, and now I fell to my knees, broken in my bloodlust.

Sensing my distress, Hercules jumped on the bed and licked my ear. I slammed the drawer shut. What a temptation to have the gun stuck in my pants, covered by my blue sweatshirt, and Bennett walking toward me.

How would I ever find my way and feel safe in this post-Perico world?

He'd been my cane.

My emotions around losing him were still raw. The past two weeks, which I'd spent mostly writing to distill my thoughts, led me to believe that forgiveness was like a road filled with craters; any slight misstep and I'd end up tossing the smoking gun behind the bushes trimmed with a barber's precision. Hercules had been helping to keep me grounded, acting as a deterrent against kissing the bullets. After all, what would he do if I went to jail?

At work, I noticed Bennett had removed Perico's name from the sign-in sheet. And next to Chuchoka's name, Bennett had written *IA* for the entire week.

"Welcome back," Bennett said, without lifting his eyes from his paperwork. His hair was uncombed. "Don't forget to buff the fourth floor."

"Did Chuchoka get hurt?" I asked with a frown.

"Yes, he took a tumble and broke his arm. Missed the last step in the stairwell. A freak accident at work, so it's an industrial accident," Bennett finally looked up at me and shook his head. "He'll be out three to four weeks and get paid for it."

"Are you okay, Mr. Bennett?" I asked, gesturing to my own hair to indicate I'd noticed an unkempt look.

"Mind your own business," he snapped.

As I stalked away, my phone buzzed. A text message. *Yoyo, call me. Urgent. Chuchoka.* I frowned.

Chuchoka? What could he want with me?

After polishing my floors, I spent the rest of the day on the fourth, one of Perico's old ones. Polishing the tiles relaxed me. It wasn't arduous work, but I had to be methodical so as not to miss a spot. Kind of like rewriting. The tiles brightened up as soon as I sprayed the wax and ran the buffer over them. It was an immediate-reward type of job, the opposite of writing. Perico told me it reminded him of how heroin had made him feel. But for me, it was like meditation. The repetition allowed me to get into a groove, and I'd compose chapters in my mind. Even if there were people walking by, I remained in a state of complete concentration while advancing over the VCT flooring. Sometimes, I'd map out an entire chapter on one floor. Then it was a matter of committing the tale to paper. As I finished polishing the fourth floor, I decided the knife had to go. Part of the healing was to shed the fear.

When I left for the day, another text from Chuchoka arrived. But before I had a chance to respond, Filomena waved from the sidewalk across the parking lot.

"Yoyo."

Filomena played a critical role in the story. That much was clear. And so I approached her, and my tongue moved without consulting me. "Would you consider reading a story I'm writing? I'll need a beta reader."

Her eyes widened with delight. "Yes. What's the story about?"

"Loyalty and forgiveness."

"Well, that sounds mysterious. What's the story's name?"

"'Lealtad.'"

"'*Lealtad*,'" she said, savoring the sound of the word. "Well, count me in. I gotta run." She turned and headed to her class, carrying a bulging backpack.

In my car, I breathed a sigh of relief. I'd begun to survive without Perico.

I drove home at a good clip, enjoying the feeling of my hair blowing to the wind's desire, despite the cold air. The stillness of the water in a large pond caught my attention for a moment.

When I parked in my driveway, I spotted Hercules on the couch, his nose peeking through the white curtains and his eyes glistening. He took off toward the entrance, and when I walked in, he barked. It wasn't a simple woof—more like a scolding. We'd both gotten used to spending more time together. I got on the floor, and we rubbed our noses and foreheads until we'd calmed down.

A sudden curiosity prompted me to grab the framed picture on the coffee table next to the couch. What had happened to Bellatrix? I'd promised Perico that I'd find her if something happened to him. It was a pledge I'd hoped not to have to follow through on. Perico had told me to ask Chuchoka for help. I suddenly remembered I'd forgotten to respond to him. Was that why he was trying to get in touch with me?

He answered on the first ring. "Yoyo," he whispered. "Can we meet?"

"Why?"

"Trust me. Do you know the arboretum? The section that goes up a hill? Meet me there before seven this evening. By the west entrance. It's empty at that time because it begins to get dark." He hung up.

My first instinct was to call back and tell him I felt sick, and something told me Perico's wish and meeting this maniac were tied together. But the park had always been a safe place for Hercules and me when we went for strolls, not counting the time when two Great Danes chased Hercules down a hill after he barked at them. His short legs had spun like those of a cartoon character before taking off after a drumroll sounded.

Before leaving, I kissed Hercules and left him with extra water and food, just in case. I also placed pee pads in the bathroom and then went across the street to put a note in Felicia's mailbox. She saw me and came out with a quizzical expression.

"It's just a note saying thank you. The chocolate you left was good, too. I appreciate them."

Coming down the steps, she smiled and said, "You're welcome. I enjoy taking care of Hercules." Her smile faded a little. "Are you okay? You look worried."

I nodded. "I am. I wish I could explain, but right now, I can't."

She began to walk toward me, but I started to back up. "Andrew, just please be safe wherever you're going."

I nodded and quickly returned to my driveway.

At the arboretum, I parked on a narrow street flanked by tall pine trees. The west entrance to the park looked desolate. I got out and was about to take off again, convinced I'd made the wrong decision, when someone clasped my arm from behind. My mouth went dry.

"Yoyo, let's walk up to the top. More privacy there."

There was no room for discussion. As we walked, I noticed his right arm was in a cast. Bennett must have been telling the truth. The long road uphill became increasingly shadowy. My breaths came a little quicker, and I inhaled the sweet aroma of the surrounding trees. The only sound was our steps biting the asphalt weaving around the hill.

As we neared the top, the budding lights of downtown Boston twinkled at us every time we made our way to the east side of the hill. All other walkers had fled.

Our flashlights carved up the enveloping darkness.

"I'll get straight to the point," Chuchoka said once we'd reached the bench at the summit. Neither of us sat. All the natural light was gone, but there was still a fleeting glow on the horizon. "I put a contract on Bennett's life. In three days, she'll cancel him. I'd do him myself, but with a broken arm, it may be a challenge."

"What?"

"Yes. It's not related to your thing." He gestured to his rear. "Not directly, anyway. Bennett tried to get me fired. Little-shit stuff." He shrugged and added, "His fault."

"My *thing*?" I spat as my anger replaced my fear.

"Perico filled me in on everything," he said casually. "At first, I couldn't understand what you did or why. Convincing the giant?" He shook his head. "That's a tall task, my friend. I think you're crazy, Yoyo, but good crazy." He smiled, perhaps for the first time in his life.

"Oh, this is getting better and better," I said, crossing my arms. "Why don't you tell me more about how I'm crazy? While you're at it, tell me more about this *thing* of mine."

He held up his hand. "Don't get upset. Anyway, Perico had a good reason to tell me. Let me explain."

For the first time, the grunt's expression resembled one of warmth. "Perico said that if something happened to him, I should look after you. 'In case Bennett feels amorous again,'" Chuchoka said with a snicker, making air quotes.

"I don't believe you," I said, while every muscle in my body tensed.

"You don't have to. But I haven't taken this trip up this hill to tell you some bullshit story, Yoyo."

I ran my fingers through my hair. "So then, why did you take this trip to this emptiness?"

"Because Perico called me from the hospital and asked me to run the errand if circumstances demanded it. I'll tell you," he said with a scoff, "Bennett would already be six feet under if he touched somebody close to me."

"You talked to Perico when he was in the hospital?" I said, getting louder and distrusting everything the man said. "He slept most of the time!"

"Yep. He made me promise to look after you. 'Look after Yoyo,' he said. Those were Perico's very last words to me."

"I can't believe this," I said, but I vaguely remembered the nurse telling me that Perico spoke with someone on the phone before I arrived that last day. The message was somewhat comforting, I had to admit, but the messenger was unreliable. On top of the hill, I felt a sense of surrealness that reminded me of that day in the hospital. "Are you playing with me?"

He smiled again. Not a jovial one. "Does it look like I play?"

The flashlight illuminated only parts of his face.

"Do you want me to dissuade you, like I did with Perico? Is that what this is about? Screw you, Chuchoka. I'm done with this." I turned to walk away.

"That's the thing. No, I don't want you to dissuade me. The contract is out. I just thought you should know. Because if the Specialist kills Bennett, I think it will affect you. And Perico told me to look after you. So this creates a bit of a conflict for me. Look, Yoyo, there's no manual for this stuff."

I stopped, turned around, and walked toward him, holding a finger up to his face. "Chuchoka, I'm gonna say something. And if you get offended, too bad."

He held up his palm. "Before you do, man, you gotta know some things. First, Perico cared about you."

"I know. That's nothing new."

Chuchoka set his flashlight on the granite seat behind us with its beam pointing to the sky. The flickering city lights rested miles away. "I don't think you understand what I'm trying to say. Your insolence—Perico didn't tolerate that from other people. What he wanted to do to Bennett was his twisted form of caring about you. But he respected your desire to not see Bennett fly off the roof. I told Perico I had a connection who'd get the job done, and that you'd never have known what happened."

My head spun. The setting disoriented me. "I don't know what to say, Chuchoka."

I sat on the cold granite seat.

"And my second point, Yoyo. Perico was sick for a long time. He had an ulcerated foot and didn't take care of his diabetes. He knew what would happen with his weak heart and all, but wanted to spare you the pain of knowing." This time, he got in my face. "'Bellatrix and Yoyo. The two loves of my life.' His words."

A shudder ran through me. And then I grabbed Chuchoka by the neck without caring about his broken arm. "Don't you play with my feelings, you bastard." We tumbled to the ground, and I felt a heavy object hit me over the head. I released my grip and sat up, wheezing.

Chuchoka's eyes looked like two coals that had been heating for hours.

"Perico told me to threaten Bennett and give him an ultimatum, if necessary," he shouted. "'You have free rein. Bennett has a daughter.' That's what he said."

I felt my face pale.

"And so I did. Give him an ultimatum, that is. I told him his dear Filomena was gone if he ever touched you again. But Bennett just couldn't help himself—he still tried to get me fired. Insane, right?"

I barely digested the flurry of words. There had been so much at play that I hadn't been aware of.

"Anyway, for years, Perico felt guilty about leaving his daughter alone when he was arrested." Then Chuchoka got right in my face again. "He wanted to die. That's why he didn't take his heart meds. I suppose the hidden skeletons were too heavy for him."

I pulled back as the information ripped through my chest like a twister. I dropped to my knees. Perico had never betrayed me. He'd been loyal to the end. I let the tears flow, and then I got up and sat next to Chuchoka on the cold granite. He patted my back.

"What do you want from me?" I muttered.

"I don't know. I promised a dying man I'd care for you, and my desire to kill Bennett is at war with that promise. I haven't slept since I called the Specialist."

I straightened and looked at Chuchoka. He looked like a ghost.

"Talk to me, Yoyo," he said. "If you don't, it's done. Bellatrix's deadly."

I blinked. "Isn't that the name of Perico's daughter?"

"Yeah, that's her. Like father, like daughter. Last night, I called her, but she didn't answer." Chuchoka nibbled on his lip.

My eyes interrogated him. In the past, I'd always had the impression that he could handle anything. Now, he seemed far from having control. Indeed, he looked disturbed. Maybe he thought Perico would haunt him.

As if reading my mind, he said, "I got desperate yesterday. That's why I called you today. You might have to talk to Bellatrix in person. After putting the contract on Bennett, I had an awful nightmare. Perico's ghost stood by my bedroom, dressed in black. I woke up screaming."

"Why me? You're the one who put the contract on Bennett."

"But you're the only one who might get her to cancel the job. Well, at least postpone it."

"Are you drunk?"

He continued, unfazed. "Tell Bellatrix your weird story and how you want to save the guy who poked you." He laughed so hard he grabbed his belly as if it hurt. "Nobody could come up with a story so wacky unless it was for real. So yeah, Bellatrix will either believe you or kill you. You'd better bring your best game. Polish your fucking story."

"Um, okay, Professor. Thanks for the advice."

He slapped my shoulder, and I felt his breath on my face. "Listen, Bellatrix isn't answering because she doesn't want to cancel the contract."

"Talking to her sounds like a surefire way for me to get canceled," I said with a scoff.

"I've got something that will help." He leaned down, and out of his right boot came a sharp object, which he placed next to my throat. Before I had time to gasp, he nicked my neck. I felt something warm running from the spot.

"What was that for?"

He chuckled. "Nobody disrespects me. Grabbing my neck? Never again. That was your one chance. I'll kill you, promise or not. I'll deal with Perico's ghost." Then he placed the dagger in my palm. It was a bold move, considering he'd nicked me. "Proof that you talked to me. Otherwise, she'll kill you right away." Then he kissed one of his fingers and put it on the spot where he cut me. "It's only a boo-boo."

"Beautiful. Guess I should go say my goodbyes to my dog."

"It's your choice. You don't have to go. To tell you the truth, it's probably pointless. This isn't the type of business transaction where you can ask for your money back."

"This is a suicide mission, and you know it."

He grabbed me by my shoulder as if we were pals. "This is your chance to prove what you believe in. Will you risk your life for the man who took your manhood? Or let him die like the pig he is?"

I dropped my chin. Writing a story was one thing, but putting the whole premise to the test with my life in the balance was something else entirely.

"It's not all bad, Yoyo. Bellatrix is stunning. Our association is strictly business, but with you, who knows? You got the looks. Now, let's see if you got the charms. And one more thing: call her the Specialist. She likes to keep her real name out of circulation, if you know what I mean."

He smirked. His face looked warped in the dim light.

"If you want to write the story, you better survive, Yoyo. If not, I'll put a flower on your grave and take your fluffy rascal. What's his name?"

The mention of my dog made my hand itch. I wanted to bury the dagger in Chuchoka's heart and twist it. I squeezed the smooth metal handle.

He passed me a leather holster. "You'll need this," he said, and then handed me a business card as well. I squinted to read the tagline. *I'll usher you into your unknown passions. The Specialist.* The address was on Beacon Street, somewhere near the Charles River, not too far from where I was learning to be a civilized man, studying the classics.

"I know I don't need to tell you not to blab about this to anyone. I'm sure you know who you're dealing with by now."

When I looked up, Chuchoka was already heading down the hill. His flashlight sliced through the darkness.

"Welcome to my world," he thundered. The macabre laughter that followed replayed in my head as I ventured down, trying to feel my way through the darkness.

Chapter 8

PAGES FOR THE PROFESSOR

Wednesday, November 6

THE DAGGER RESTED ON the passenger seat. My makeshift business card for Bellatrix. It was a work of true craftsmanship, and it lusted for flesh. While my left hand held the steering wheel, my right traveled over the soft leather of the scabbard. It felt like flower petals with a long stem. And just like that, I realized I didn't matter to Chuchoka. And that was the difference between Perico and him. Nevertheless, Chuchoka needed to know he could trust me before allowing me to represent him—to know that I wasn't going to piss down my leg. A task impossible to determine over the phone.

It seemed that Chuchoka feared Bellatrix, the minister of death—the Specialist. Yet the failure to keep a promise made to a dying man clearly petrified him. The more I thought about it, the more I realized how superstitious Chuchoka was. One day, he'd come to work dressed in black, saying his long-gone lover had ordered him to wear black for a month to regain his youthful virility. This was unusual for him because he liked to dress in lively colors. But after three weeks, he decided that he'd had enough and strapped a flamboyant yellow apron around his waist while cooking a steak at home.

"The apron caught on fire, but nothing else burned," he'd told me solemnly at work the next day. "I won't defy the spirits anymore." My first reaction was to laugh, but I did my best to contain my emotions by massaging my cheeks.

A stream of red lights blinked before me on Blue Hill Avenue, so I took the back streets. Time was of the essence. I needed to shower and change before visiting Bellatrix.

My life depended on making a phenomenal first impression.

When I entered, Felicia's peppermint scent hung over the living room. She hadn't waited until morning to check on Hercules, but he seemed content, so I was grateful. In my room, I placed the dagger in my backpack. I could always say it was for a research project for school, but, of course, that was a far-fetched excuse.

The first time I'd prevented Bennett's murder, I'd had weeks of back-and-forth on the roof, which culminated at Perico's apartment that evening. This time, there was no yoyoing.

I showered and then ironed my favorite shirt, which was light blue. I smoothed all the creases and spent extra time on the neck and cuffs. Hercules came by and attempted to jump on the bed, but I made a guttural noise, and he got the message. I sprayed a mist of my best cologne on the shirt before putting it on.

Next, I pulled on black jeans and slipped into my brown Italian leather shoes.

Before leaving, I hugged Hercules for a long time. I took the little bandanna from around his neck, smelled it, and then put it in the back pocket of my jeans. I also called Mom and left a simple message: "I miss you." If I'd said "I love you," she'd have sensed something was awry.

I hadn't uttered those words since Jenny died. I'd said them to Mom right after the funeral. She'd just raised her palm and replied, "I don't need that right now." The interaction had left me feeling immensely alone, as if I'd lost both women. That night, in an attempt to feel numb, I'd knelt in the snowy backyard, with the wind howling around me until my skin screamed.

I saw the sheers move in Felicia's place as I got into my car. While driving, I kept my finger away from the radio dial. Quiet helped me to think and soothed my mind. A person could die. Bennett was someone who'd hurt me, but he was still a human being. Soon, my shirt was damp.

I parked outside the address on Beacon Street, and before leaving the vehicle, I said aloud, "Who's walking in here, Andrew or Yoyo?"

Andrew had a greater need, the redemptive kind, but Yoyo wanted to explore his evil inclinations. He could change course at any moment. It was what people had begun to expect from him.

With a deep breath, I grabbed my bag and emerged onto the street. From outside, the building looked like any other on the block. Tan, or a shade of it, was the preferred color in the neighborhood. In this case, it was elegant and blended well without raising any suspicions. At the same time, the red door appeared more enticing. A barefoot young woman dressed in a white tunic opened the heavy door. I gave her Bellatrix's card.

"The Specialist's an excellent choice," she said with a flirtatious smile.

She ushered me into a plush room with plenty of couches and subdued lighting. I tapped my fingers to the soft music. "First time?" she asked as several women who looked quite different from each other appeared. The warm and inviting atmosphere made me feel relaxed in a way I hadn't been in a while.

A plump man rested on one of the couches. He held his wide-brimmed hat with both hands, and his eyes bulged. He pointed at a woman with hair to her waist. She grabbed his chubby hand and led him upstairs, where they disappeared behind a green door.

"I'm the Specialist," said a low, smooth voice behind me.

I spun to face her and realized she was the mysterious woman I'd seen near Perico's hospital room and at his funeral. I couldn't believe I hadn't put two and two together earlier.

She nodded. I tried not to stare. Chuchoka had been right about her beauty. It was evident even through all her makeup, which was equally mesmerizing. She had dark penciled eyebrows, and her eyelashes held a delicate layer of glittering gold, which complemented her greenish eyes. Her lips, a glossy pink, had an immaculate delineation.

"I'm Andrew," I said, as we settled on a love seat, "but they call me Yoyo at work." I played with the ends of my hair, feeling stupid for making such a pitiful introduction. She looked like a woman who could toy with any man's carefully crafted line. I clasped my left hand to stop the fidgeting. "I have something delicate to discuss with you."

"Discuss?" she said and gave me a look that suggested she was ready for action, not talking.

"Are you the Specialist?" I said, moving closer to her. "The one that makes people go away?"

Her head moved back, but her eyes sparkled. "Why don't we go upstairs," she said, standing. Her long dark hair moved like the branches of a willow tree swaying in a soft breeze.

"We'll have more privacy there," she said.

I followed her up the stairs, grateful to have a moment to compose myself. Her feet in high heels made her taller than I was. She moved with sureness and elegance; her silk dress caressed her ankles.

We passed the green door as well as a purple one. Her door was the color of a golden bullet casing.

"Chuchoka, he sent me here," I blurted as soon as she closed the door behind us. I needed to state my case before I forgot why I was there. "He's having second thoughts about the contract."

She looked me straight in the eye, and for a moment, I recognized an element I'd seen in Perico's gaze. Moving close, she nibbled my earlobe. "The short man doesn't work with emissaries," she said with a growl.

In my mind, I'd established how to tell Bellatrix the story and make my argument compelling. But her presence had disarmed me. Everything about her left me feeling vulnerable. I knew she saw it in my eyes. She'd shifted without effort between her personas—the escort and the killer. Chuchoka had failed to mention the former.

"He tried to reach you," I said.

"So, you know what I do besides this little entertainment thing?" She kissed my other ear. I closed my eyes to hide how much power she had over me.

"Chuchoka told me—" I cleared my throat as her lips played with my neck, and my whole body caught fire. "He thought you might hear what I have to say before killing me."

"He said that?" She grinned. "Your name is Andrew, right?"

I nodded. I was Andrew, not Yoyo. Yoyo wanted to, perhaps, take part in a murder. Her fingers glided over my chest. Then she ran a long fingernail across my neck as if slashing it.

"I knew your father," I said, trying to gain some control.

A shadow passed over her gaze, and she blinked. Then she looked me up and down, and fluttered her eyelashes, taking back the upper hand.

"You really came here only to talk? Shame." Her scent made me want to breathe until my lungs could take in no more air.

"Believe me," I said, "I'd love to enjoy the moment." I cleared my throat again. "I worked with Perico, your father, and for a long time, he looked after me." I paused, then quickly added, "Not that I asked him to do that."

She put her index finger over my lips, grabbed me by the shirt, and said, "Here, we do all the talking between the sheets."

With that, she pushed me onto the soft bed and lay beside me with her clothes on. "That way, it stays confidential."

I nodded, powerless, staring at the ceiling, trying to stay focused on my task. I couldn't remember the last time I'd felt this way around a woman.

"Most men who come here aren't good-looking," she said, looking at me as if searching for my deepest thoughts. "You're the exception. Solace comes to the weary."

"I'm writing a book," I said, still staring at the ceiling.

"A book? But of course you are," she said, and flipped one of my hands back and forth in hers. "These aren't the hands of a laborer." She ran her fingers over my face and slid them down to my chest, letting them rest there. "You have a passionate heart, Andrew. I'm an expert at untangling men's secret desires. You can call me a specialist in that regard. I'm sure that's what you heard about me."

She was giving me a way out. I didn't take it.

I was no longer Yoyo but an assertive Andrew. "I am writing a story hoping that the villain, Bennett, will read it and change his ways when he realizes someone saved his life not once but twice. The idea is that his daughter will read the story, recognize her dad in it, and give it to him to read."

"You're a romantic," she said. I looked at her, and her expression said it all. My effort was a futile one. "That's Andrew, the romantic, doing the talking."

I looked back at the ceiling, feeling even more exposed than before. I needed to change my strategy again. "I have proof that I spoke with Chuchoka. It's in my bag."

Bellatrix retrieved the bulky bag from the white chair beside the window, which was covered by long gold curtains, and ambled back toward the bed while searching it. Then I noticed the rubber tree beside the chair. Now, I was sure she was Perico's daughter.

"What do we have here?" She lay back on the bed, removed the dagger from its scabbard, and placed it between us. "Do you know what you're doing?" she asked ominously. "Coming here with a weapon and a strange story?"

I met her now-cold gaze and once again thought of Perico. Though her expression reminded me that she didn't care about me, as Perico had.

Sensing my life was in danger, I started babbling. "When your father was on his deathbed, he made Chuchoka promise to look after me," I said, gasping for air. "Chuchoka knows that if Bennett dies a violent death, it will affect me profoundly. Even though Bennett might well deserve it."

She picked up the blade and then slowly put it back in the scabbard, toying with me once again.

"Will you consider canceling the hit?" I asked. My words were softer than the blue velvet bag at home. "I don't want to see him killed. It will make my healing impossible." It was my last attempt.

Just then, a woman screamed. We both looked in the direction of the door, and without hesitation Bellatrix grabbed the dagger and ran out of the room. I followed her to the hall, where she pounded on a locked purple door with the smooth metallic head of the dagger. Several men and women in their undergarments peered out of other doors.

A tall man dressed in black strode with heavy steps into the hall and pounded on the purple door. His tone was commanding.

The voice that replied from behind the locked door sounded familiar. My jaw dropped. "It's Bennett," I whispered to Bellatrix. "The man I'm trying to save."

"You mean the prey has come to the lion's den?"

"Please don't," I said, with panic churning in my gut.

"I'll take care of this, Freddy," Bellatrix said to the tall man.

"If you need me to open the door, let me know," he replied, giving Bellatrix a paternal look before disappearing.

"He takes care of the building and keeps it running smoothly," she said, turning to me when she saw my questioning eyes.

"A pimp?"

"No. Freddy's not that type of man."

I heard a woman's voice from behind the door. "Jack's calming down. Right, honey? Everything is fine, girl."

"If anything happens, call me."

I followed Bellatrix back to her room. "That's the man you want to protect?" she said, closing the door. All the flirtatiousness had fled from her voice.

"I'm afraid so."

She sat on the king-size bed and patted the spot beside her. "Talk to me, Andrew. Make sense of this because, right now, it doesn't."

I sat where she'd gestured. "Well, it's a senseless situation. It's almost impossible to explain."

"Try. We have some time."

"I did try to tell you, but you think I'm a romantic."

She made a circular motion with her hand, urging me on. Reminding me of the professor, it put me at ease.

I shifted my body toward her. "Years ago, I got caught in a snowstorm while driving. My younger sister was in the car. Short story—I lost control and hit a tree. She died on impact. My mom never recovered, and I left home to find peace. I'm still trying to find it. I'm still working through the guilt."

Bellatrix leaned back and rested her head on the pillow but never took her eyes off me. She tapped the pillow, and I laid my head on it as well.

"I ended up moving to Mattapan, not far from your father's place, and got a job at the university, where I eventually met Chuchoka and Perico after some time had gone by. Then, I was paired with Perico for a couple of weeks. He was a little rough on me at first. Wanted to show me who was boss, but I never complained. Most of the people were afraid of him, but I wasn't."

"No?"

I shook my head. "I mean, he was massive, like Freddy. A true sight and dangerous, too. In my right mind, I should have been scared. But my problems were much greater, and I was numb to pain and fear for a while."

"I suppose you were brave," she said, caressing my neck.

"The university seemed like a good place to start over. I decided to get a degree—I needed something to focus my energy on after my sister's death. Anyway, Bennett was always tough on me. He needed to feel like he had power over people, but Perico handled him well, and Chuchoka? No explanation needed, right?"

She laughed. "Go on."

I chuckled, then sobered. "One day, Bennett called me to the basement, and when I walked into the room, he knocked me out from behind. He, well . . ."

In my silence, Bellatrix's eyes opened wide, and she seemed to connect the dots in her mind. She pulled me close. I felt I'd made some progress in my recovery, but as I sunk into Bellatrix's arms, I realized I was far from cured. My pain poured on her bosom.

"So," Bellatrix said softly, "you feel that if I kill Bennett, his death will add to the guilt you already feel because of your sister's death? Did I get it right?"

I nodded as tears dripped from my eyes. "If you kill Bennett, I'll never be able to fully heal."

Bellatrix stood, dagger in hand, and marched to the door, which she stabbed with all her strength, making me jump. She pried out the dagger and stabbed it twice more into the door. The third stab was a little lower.

"Sorry," she said, returning to the bed to lie beside me. She exhaled. "Your story brought back memories."

"Some days, that's what I want to do to Bennett."

To my surprise, she blinked, and tears ventured down her cheeks. "Tell me about my dad."

I fought the urge to wipe away her tears. Despite the sadness in her eyes, her expression was scarier than Perico's had ever been.

"Your dad protected me the best he knew how," I said. "But he couldn't have foreseen the attack."

Bellatrix tensed. "Bennett's a predator."

I nodded. I'd always suspected he'd recognized I was wounded, though I'd never told him about Jenny's death. "Perico and I discussed killing Bennett. And Perico was always ready to do it. I wasn't." I grimaced.

"You've been going through hell," she said, nodding.

"Yeah, and if I don't prevent his death, I'll be in this inferno for the rest of my life. I don't think I could withstand that."

She lowered her eyes and then looked at me again. "I understand a little better now."

"I'm glad. This is difficult to explain."

"But forgive me, Andrew. I'm still confused," she said, pursing her lips. "Chuchoka's request has nothing to do with you—not directly, anyway."

"You're right. But now that Chuchoka's told me about it, I can't cross my arms and pretend I don't know. Isn't averting a murder always someone's business? Don't you think every person deserves a chance to change?"

"Perhaps in the world you live in," Bellatrix said, without emotion. "In my world, you fuck up, you die."

I peered at Bellatrix, who seemed calm again. She was both methodical in her reasoning and skilled in extracting secrets. I felt I could tell her anything.

"It's hell," I said. "Having your life linked to the man you despise. But 'in my world,' as you say, despising someone doesn't justify murdering them."

"I do what the customer wants. Of course, I have feelings about things, but it's a job like any other."

"It's that simple?"

"It is and it's not. Nothing is simple or complicated in itself. It's about the meaning we give it."

"I know I can't prevent you from carrying out your contract, but I'm pleading with you," I said, trying to keep the desperation I felt out of my voice. "You don't know me, and I can't expect your loyalty, but I can see that you have compassion. Chuchoka, you know him better than I do. He's not loyal to me, either, but he was loyal to your father, and he's worried about breaking his promise to him—to look out for me. He gave an oath to a dying man. Death means something, even if life doesn't."

Her face dissolved into a river of melancholy.

"I can understand. I'm not a machine."

Once again, fighting the urge to comfort her, I said gently, "Tell me a little about your background."

She smiled.

"Well, Freddy, the man you saw in the hall, he took care of me sometime after Dad went to jail."

I frowned in confusion, but she continued. "I was also attacked by a man, shortly after Dad went to jail, and afterward I ran off. My mom had mental health issues and was admitted to a hospital after she gave birth to my sister—she was adopted, too—different family than me."

My heart ached for her, but I kept quiet.

"Freddy saw me crying at a bus stop and sat beside me. He asked where my parents were and what I was doing out so late. When he quizzed me if I wanted him to call the police, I cried even louder. Then he said, 'Listen, you can spend the night in my guest room, but tomorrow, we need to find a place appropriate for a little girl like you. Tomorrow, we'll go to the police station. My wife died a couple of months ago, and I live alone, but you need a proper family.'"

I bit my tongue. "So did Freddy end up taking you to the police station?"

"He wanted to, but I begged him not to. I'd just watched the police arrest my dad in our home. I didn't exactly trust them. One day, I followed Freddy to work. When he got home, I asked him if I could earn my keep. He didn't want to allow it, but I forced his hand. I told him I'd go stand on a corner otherwise."

Bellatrix stood again and paced, stopping by the window to stroke the leaves of the rubber tree. I thought of Perico standing by the window that rainy night before he commuted Bennett's sentence.

"I'll hold off on the contract for now," she said, with a businesslike tone. She held up a hand to stop me from expressing my gratitude. "But I have to tell you, I don't think it's a wise idea. He comes here every week and isn't nice to the girls. He hurts people, Andrew. When will you let him go?"

"Don't you think I want to?"

"You put yourself at risk coming here tonight. Don't think I didn't consider getting rid of you." Her face became grave. "People have died for less than what you did tonight."

I put my hands in my pockets to hide the trembling. Right then, I realized Chuchoka hadn't expected me to survive. And if I was dead, he'd be freed from his promise to Perico. Sending me here had been a macabre machination worthy of Bennett himself.

"I propose we put Bennett to the test," she said.

I narrowed my eyes in question.

"Your book. Finish it soon. Then, ensure Bennett reads it, and we'll see if he changes. We'll give him that chance. But if he doesn't, he'll meet the true Specialist."

I'd gotten what I wanted—for now.

"I have to work now, Andrew. You need to go." She tapped the nightstand and then lifted two fingers.

I dropped two hundred dollars on the nightstand and went to the door. As I was about to leave, I caught sight of a rubber tree leaf on the floor. I picked it up. "A souvenir, my lady."

"My door is always open, Andrew. And if you want to come over and not talk so much, even better."

I smiled and met her gaze. "I'll keep your offer in mind."

"You do that."

Closing the door behind me, I saw the plump man exit the green door holding his hat. His tie hung around his neck, and he looked as if he didn't know where he was. I grabbed him by the arm and led him downstairs. As I did so, I noted the thick silver ring on his left hand.

I tried to make conversation, but his mind was elsewhere.

When we reached my car, I retrieved my hankie and some hand sanitizer. I doused the handkerchief and handed it to him so he could clean the lipstick off his face.

"Thank you," he said. "My wife's going to kill me. We had a fight, and I went out to clear my mind."

"I'd say your mind is clear," I said, patting his back. "Don't worry, buddy. I went through something similar, but the difference is that my companion will kiss me when I get home. He's a dog," I said, hoping to make him laugh.

His eyes widened. "If I could only have your luck."

"Take care of yourself and wait before you drive. If I were a cop, I'd stop you."

It was late when I got home, but as I got out of the car, I thought I saw movement behind Felicia's sheers, so I waved in her direction. I heard Hercules scratching the door. He jumped and barked at me when I opened it, and I hugged him as if I'd been away for six months.

I let him out through the back door and then sat on the steps overlooking the brownish grass and the dead flowers enclosed within my fence. My idea had become real. I was drafting a story to save my attacker. Until now, I hadn't actually had to give it to anyone but Professor Levine. Now, the story would serve a real purpose. The grade was the least of my concerns.

Twice now, I'd saved Bennett with my voice. Now, I had to do it with my words on the page. No more yoyoing. Deciding to forgive Bennett had been the right choice.

Hercules and I cuddled on the couch for a few minutes, and he kept sniffing my clothes. Bellatrix's picture stared back at us. She wasn't that little girl anymore. Perico would have been distraught if he'd known how much his actions had affected her life.

I closed my eyes, and the plump man came into my mind. I couldn't help but grin a little. I envied his willingness to abandon himself for pleasure. I supposed I needed a bit of that.

While I tossed and turned, Bellatrix paraded near my pillow. She wore her long flowing dress, and her hair was curled.

A dagger cuddled her thigh. Finally, unable to sleep, I wandered to the kitchen and put the rubber tree's leaf into a water-filled glass jar on the windowsill.

I'd never interacted with a woman in Bellatrix's profession before—both of them. But it was her kindness and understanding that caught my attention.

Don't mix up your feelings, I thought. *She's a murderess.*

Chapter 9

Thursday, November 7

EARLY THE NEXT MORNING, while the first light sifted through the curtains, I called Bennett on his cell phone. "I don't feel well today. Sorry for not calling earlier."

Bennett mumbled an unintelligible profanity and hung up. I looked at my phone, surprised at the venom. In his defense, his voice sounded tired after his night behind the purple door.

It was time to shift my perspective when it came to him. I'd acted like he controlled my life—the fear and anger—but he would continue to do so only if I allowed him to. I chose to stay after the attack because defeating Bennett's evil became my mission. Today would be a day of healing and self-empowerment. I took a long shower, and as the water ran, I told my soul to let every drop of water cleanse my pain and carry it away into the drain so it would never return.

Professor Levine came to mind. He'd said something to the effect of making my characters come alive. If I could do that, I could bring healing to my life. I was tired of playing the victim. It was time for my rebirth, both on the page and in real life.

My bell rang, and I went to the door wrapped in my large towel, with my chest bare. Felicia smiled and touched her hair, though every strand was perfectly in place.

I invited her in, and she stood next to the piano, facing the window overlooking the driveway.

"Are you okay?" she asked. "I don't want to pry, but your face yesterday . . ." She paused. "Your expression was ghastly. Anyway, I'm sorry for coming unannounced."

She passed her fingers over the piano book for beginners.

"Have a seat. I was about to get dressed."

I gestured to the couch before heading to the bedroom to throw on some clothes. I heard Felicia talking to Hercules.

When I returned, the rascal was belly up on the couch beside her.

"Are you in some kind of trouble?" she asked, and shifted her focus from Hercules to me.

Her gaze veered toward Bellatrix's picture. Felicia had seen the picture before, given that she'd looked after Hercules several times.

"Yeah," I said with a shrug. "I'm dealing with some stuff."

"Anything I can help with?"

"I'd have to kill you if I told you about any of it," I said but smiled.

She looked startled but then laughed.

"Someday, I'll tell you. Thank you for taking good care of my baby."

She nodded and stood. "I need to get to work," she said, and apologized again for her intrusion. Felicia laughed nervously as I accompanied her to the door. "Whenever you're ready, I'd love to hear about what might cause my demise."

"You will."

She noticed my neck. "That's a nasty cut you have there." She took a hankie from her purse and pressed it against the wound. "Keep it."

Her scent put me at ease.

"Okay, Felicia."

I watched her drive away in her sports car.

"I think she was flirting with me," I said to Hercules.

There was no doubt she was a great woman and without any apparent complications, like Bellatrix's. What a daring thought. Bellatrix. They were both equally beautiful. But I didn't want to hide anything from the woman I chose. And how could a woman accept a man who had suffered such an indignity?

Hercules barked, as if in agreement. Minutes later, I stood in the kitchen as the coffee machine sputtered, and soon, the drips became a steady stream of liquid. After filling a mug and bringing it to my mouth, I inhaled and thought about Greenfield.

Since Jenny's death, Mom and I had sporadic conversations, chats that didn't require us to confront our unresolved emotions. Often, Mom would land some kind of blow, and I'd say something insensitive as a response. But to heal from the brutal attack, I'd need to reveal all that hid in the crevices of my heart. Mom was the first step in the reconciliation I craved.

Hercules whined for a treat. After giving him one, I looked out of the kitchen window. A red cardinal perched on the empty branch of the cherry tree. During the summer the colorful leaves protected my horseshoe-like patch of grass from the blistering midday rays. The beauty of the scene reminded me of how much Jenny loved to paint. I'd been trying not to think about the good memories of her. It was too painful. But for healing to arrive, the memories had to surface.

I picked up my phone. Mom answered on the first ring. "I want to come home for the weekend. Is that okay?"

"I'll fix the tuna casserole you and Jenny used to fight over. Remember?"

"Yes," I said, stunned that she hadn't needed any convincing.

After I hung up, a lonesome tear hit the floor. Already there was progress.

That evening, my bell rang. I wasn't expecting any visitors. On my way to the door, I restrained my irrepressible desire to run and grab the baseball bat in the closet. I peered into the peephole.

Chuchoka stood on my porch dressed in black and wearing sunglasses, even though the last sunrays had fled. His cast was gone.

When I opened the door, he smirked, and I did my best to hide my rage. "How did you know where I live?"

"I've known for a long time," he said with a shrug.

"So, what can I do for you?"

"You're not going to invite me in?" he said with an air of self-confidence, as if something had already tilted the outcome in his favor.

I opened the door only a little farther, but Chuchoka pushed his way in like a snake slithering between rocks. "You didn't call to tell me how it went, Yoyo," he said with a threatening tone. He turned around the room, observing everything, trying to decipher me based on my choice of furniture.

"Right. You were not expecting my call. But I'm still alive."

Hercules approached, sniffing. Hyperalert. He'd always been able to read my discomfort.

"I know what you did," I said. "And if my mom didn't pray for me every morning, I probably would have died last night."

"No hard feelings, right?" Chuchoka said before settling on the couch.

I scoffed.

"I'm thirsty. You got a beer?"

Hercules jumped on the couch as well but kept his distance. When the uninvited guest tried to pet him, he growled, showing teeth.

"Bellatrix is pretty," Chuchoka said as I entered the kitchen to get the beer, scratching my neck. "Isn't she?"

I heard Hercules snarl.

"She is, but that's not the point," I called, and felt something on my neck. I returned with the beer and a mug of reheated coffee for me. Handing him the drink, I shook my head and sneered. "Walking in there with a dagger? What an idiot."

I sat at the other end of the couch, took a sip, and pressed Felicia's hankie to my wound because my finger had a speckle of blood.

Chuchoka pursed his lips. "You should be more careful when you shave. Is that Bellatrix's hankie?"

His lascivious eyes widened with envy.

"Why do you care?" I said, looking at him with revulsion.

"I guess you told Bellatrix a marvelous story. That's good, right? You got what you wanted." Hercules barked at him. "What did Bellatrix say?" There was a note of impatience in his tone now.

"She agreed to hold off on the job until I finish the story. And, of course, get Bennett to read it."

"Nice, nice. Bennett gets the chance to breathe a little more, huh?" He stood and paced for a moment. Then he curled his lip and said, "He's gonna get killed anyway."

Observing me, he continued. "What I mean is that he won't change. Perico knew that."

He entered the dining room, where a mirror with an ornate golden frame hung on the wall. He contemplated himself, then looked at me in the glass.

"Stop it," I said, smacking the coffee table with my open hand. "I'm tired of preventing you from committing murder."

Chuchoka returned to the couch with a tense face. He ignored Hercules's growls.

"Let's pretend I'm not having any impure thoughts this evening," he said. "How would you know that Bennett has changed?" His forehead furrowed. "Because he won't try to take your pants down again?" With that, he roared and clapped twice. I had to restrain my miniature dog from attacking him.

"It's a good question," I said, aware of his provocation. "A fair one." Chuchoka looked disappointed that his poisonous speech hadn't inflicted the intended damage this time. Unease spread across his face. "I don't know the answer," I continued. "Bellatrix told me he frequents her establishment every week and isn't nice to the girls. Maybe we can monitor his conduct there."

This time, I stood to pace. I moved back and forth between the piano and Perico's rubber tree on the other side of the room.

"We need meat," Chuchoka said, standing as well. "I know this kid, good-looking like you. He wants a job. I can steer him in Bennett's direction. But he's tough. Nothing like you."

I laughed in disbelief. "You come into my house uninvited. Then you insult me. And now you're planning to put someone else in danger." The anger was already back. "I am not cool with this. I won't be part of it."

He sat on the piano bench and struck a few keys. "What do you propose?"

"I told you, let's monitor his conduct at the bordello after he reads the story."

"You really think your story will render fruit?" His words crawled to me over his derisive look.

Hercules growled again. "Chuchoka, I've got things to do now. Thank you for stopping by, but don't make it a habit."

As he walked to the door, he glanced at Hercules and narrowed his eyes.

I refused to let him continue that apparent train of thought. "You can threaten me. I don't care at this point." And at that moment, I realized it was true, since, in the last months, I had survived rape, faced constant danger . . . "But Hercules . . . Don't cross that line."

He searched my eyes to see if I'd follow through. Then, without another word, he turned around and slammed the door behind him.

I let out a long breath, and Hercules looked at me.

Chapter 10

Saturday, November 9

IT WAS A SOLID two-hour drive to Greenfield. The first two miles of the trip were on River Street, the same route I'd once taken to Perico's apartment. Most of the two-family homes had siding instead of painted clapboards. Some lucky residents had rectangular patches of neatly cut grass. Others, the unlucky ones, waded through knee-high weeds between asphalt and ready-to-fall fences.

I opened the passenger window for Hercules, who sat beside me. The word *flair* popped into my mind as his long, unruly hair fluttered in the wind. After I passed the street leading to Perico's former apartment building, my mind flew in multiple directions, like a piñata struck with full force. I'd been thinking about visiting the cemetery with Mom, but perhaps it was premature. We needed to reconcile first. But what if Mom didn't forgive me? Plus, her saying the words and actually releasing me from blame were two different things. Maybe it was easier to cling to guilt.

I still hadn't admitted to Mom I'd been driving too fast the morning of the accident. I'd already done wrong in her eyes. Two wrongs? I didn't want to think about that. The police hadn't been able to reconstruct the accident, given the heavy snow. Thankfully, alcohol had been far from my mouth that day.

I'd also never told Mom about the black widow spider. She would have thought I was trying to avoid responsibility.

I shuddered at the memory of seeing the distinctive red mark on the back of the creepy stranger, confident of her poison. And I'd become distracted by my sister's panic.

Since that day, I'd carried not only the weight of Jenny's death but also the weight of my survivor's guilt. The older brother, I should have died. So I stopped celebrating my birthday. I'd inhaled and exhaled. I'd consumed food and water. But I hadn't been fully alive.

The trip passed quickly. The pine trees welcomed me to the mountain leading up to Greenfield. I reached the house to find it shrouded by bushes, which had also laid siege to the front windows with their unruly tentacles. Spiderwebs hung in the corners of the front door like ornaments, and the grass in the front yard was unkempt.

The house appeared to be suspended in time.

I knocked on the side door, where the driveway was, and soon heard Mom coming down the steps. She opened the door, and we contemplated each other for a moment. Then we both broke down. I embraced her for a long time. Aging had come to her, and she physically looked well, but her scurrying eyes gave me a sensation that something was unsolved between us.

"I have company in the car," I said as I pulled away.

She frowned and tilted her head but followed me back to the vehicle.

I opened the door and let Hercules jump out, and once on the ground, he ran in spurts, not knowing which way to go, stopping occasionally to sniff and piss.

"His name is Hercules."

Kneeling, Mom called to him. Eventually, he came to her, and in one fluid motion, he put his paws on her knees and slurped her face.

"Hah," she squealed. "You never said you had a dog. Why?" She stood and smacked my arm.

"I need to keep some secrets from you."

"Secrets? How silly you are."

Hercules led the way into the house as if he'd done so a hundred times. Climbing the stairs that led from the entryway to the main floor, I caught sight of Jenny's self-portrait on the wall, staring at me with those glittering brown eyes. It was an accomplished portrait, so much so that Mom had bought Jenny all the materials she needed after she saw her talent. I tripped and landed on all fours. Mom burst into laughter.

"Your little dog managed the stairs like a pro, and you—"

"Thanks, Mom. Thanks."

Empty tuna cans littered the counter, and the boiled peas were cooling in a strainer in the sink.

"We'll eat early, okay?"

The interior of the house was the opposite of the exterior. Inside, on the first floor, everything was spotless and in order. The wooden floors glistened, and the house smelled fresh. My heart raced as I walked on the wide planks of knotty pine, taking in the home in which the four of us had once been a family.

"Does it look different?" she said.

I hadn't felt my opinion mattered for a long time, especially at work, and her question made me feel welcomed. And maybe this was her desire to reconcile, however crowded by other deep emotions. Yet there was an ambivalence with the house—the unkempt exterior and the sparkling floors.

I lowered my backpack to the living room floor and helped set the table for our meal.

Mom got a dish out for Hercules, and after devouring his portion of tuna casserole, he rolled on the area rug next to the kitchen until he tired. He finished by rubbing his dirty snout on the carpet. Mom opened her mouth but said nothing.

Part of me was overcome by curiosity and wanted to go upstairs; the other part dreaded those nine steps. I'd have to pass Jenny's room to get to mine. I hoped Mom had closed the door.

Enjoy Mom's company and reminisce, I told myself, and set about engaging in small talk.

The giant casserole dish was half-full when we finished eating, even though I'd eaten a double portion. We both stared at it as silence descended over the table. Drawings that Jenny had done as a little girl were stuck to the fridge doors, wrinkled. Yellowing. A framed picture of the two of us sat on the counter next to the fridge.

I cleared my throat. "Why don't you pay somebody to clean up the front of the house?"

"Keeps everybody away from me. I need the space." She grabbed my hand, and her long, elegant fingers caressed mine. "Would you like a cup of tea?"

I nodded, and soon the teakettle began its song.

There was still an abyss between us, but at least we were here, sitting in front of each other for the first time in years.

The kitchen table overlooked the backyard, with its tall maple and pine trees. French doors led to the rear deck, which appeared ready to collapse. Pieces of it were missing. Mom had put a chair in front of the doors, likely to remind herself not to step out.

"How long have you had him?" she said, returning to the table with our tea and looking at Hercules stretched out on the rug as if it had always been his.

"Several years. I don't count them anymore."

"How come?"

"What's the point?"

I fidgeted with the saucer as I held my steaming cup of tea. The vapor rose between our gazes. I blew on it gently.

"I have one question for you, son. Why stay at a place that hurt you so badly? After what happened to you at work at the hands of that awful man—I mean, you can go and study at any place. You can work at any place. I don't understand. That's all I'm saying."

"I posed the same argument to myself many times."

"Then leave, baby."

I met her gaze. "I left this place a long time ago. And what's solved? The problem remained."

A shadow passed over her face. "But it's a completely different situation. It's family. Families are complex, Andrew."

She was right about that. "Let's say that I leave work and school. I'd still be wounded wherever I went. And deep in my heart, I'd feel I acted like a coward."

"No, son. No. It's self-preservation."

"Sure, Mom. Whatever you call it. I'm not buying it. I'm tired of running. No more. You might not understand it, but for the first time, I'm showing love to myself. The practical kind."

"I hear you, son, but you're dealing with a violent man. There's no telling what could happen."

"Conflict is always like that."

"I just want you to be safe. Mothers tend to protect. Sometimes, that means telling your kid to put on his running shoes."

I felt a lump form in my throat. When I was younger, I'd always felt she was controlling. So had Jenny. Now, I saw love behind the need to protect.

"I understand, but can you trust me?"

"I'll try."

I decided to try putting it in a context that would resonate with her. "Listen, you always say go and date." I exhaled and got close to her face. "Do you know what being raped does to a man's head?"

She swallowed but spoke steadily. "No, I don't."

"It made me feel filthy, but more than that, it stole my confidence. Men need to have confidence to approach women. I need to regain that trust in who I am, and one way of doing this is to fight this battle in the way that I choose. And I've chosen to write a story. It's my way of winning without ending up in hell—or jail—for killing a person." I gave a little shrug. "It's unusual, I'll give you that. But it's what I've decided to do. I'm using my brain instead of my fists. There's no honor in murder, Mom."

The tears came out of nowhere. Hercules sprung up from the rug and ran to me. Mom pulled me up into an embrace.

"I need to heal," I said, with my face in her hair. "Can you understand that?"

Mom didn't say a word, but I could feel her nodding.

"I want to heal from what Bennett did to me, and—you may not want to hear this—but from the guilt I feel over Jenny's death."

She pulled back, rolled her eyes, and folded her arms.

I felt my chest getting tight. "I came here to discuss everything that happened on that awful day. I want us to move forward with our lives."

"There you go again." With that, she grabbed a dirty dish and hurled it against the wall. It shattered, and the green peas scattered across the floor.

I jumped up.

"Are you planning to make me feel guilty for Jenny's death for the rest of my life?" I shouted back. My whole body shook. "Is that your pleasure?" I dropped my voice. "You forbade Jenny to go out with that guy, Munroe—and never explained it, Mom. She never forgave you. You did the same thing with Dad without any explanation. Didn't you?"

Mom stared at me with a stony face. Then she grabbed the sponge from the sink and moved toward the stove. But I yanked it from her hand and tossed the green-and-yellow monster back into the sink.

"If you don't forgive me, you'll lose me, too."

With a shriek, she pounced on my chest with ferocity. It was as if her own blender of emotions suddenly had no top. Feeling her body slacken, I lowered her to the floor to find her breathing but unconscious.

"Mom, wake up, please." I touched her face, and Hercules licked it and whimpered.

I carried her to the couch in the living room and knelt beside her while Hercules jumped up and lay at her feet. She slept for several hours, but she began to wake up slowly.

"Help me to my room," she said, slurring.

I draped her arm over my neck and guided her up. Hercules trailed us. There was a small den at the top of the nine steps. To the left, the long hallway led to the bedrooms. Mom had closed the first one, Jenny's room. My door was ajar. Mom's bedroom was the last one, with an open door. She still seemed dazed but began to wake up.

Back downstairs, I let Hercules out to tour Mom's plants. I did the dishes and sat at the kitchen table, feeling stunned. Perhaps it had been wrong of me to be so blunt with her. But my mouth spoke without permission after the long moratorium.

I slept as if I hadn't in years, without waking once.

In the morning, the aroma of coffee roused me. Then I heard Mom's voice.

"Andrew," Mom called from downstairs. "Breakfast is ready, honey."

I blinked slowly, but Hercules sprang up and charged out of the room. I threw on my clothes and intended to go downstairs, but small steps led me to Jenny's door. My curiosity overpowered my fear.

The room had a musty scent. There were cobwebs on the windows. I tore them down. Then my gaze landed on a rectangular wooden box with no dust. Without hesitation, I opened it and found a stack of letters. I lifted the top one and at once recognized the fancy penmanship. I knew the subject of the letters—John Munroe, the object of Jenny's love.

Mom called my name again, this time from the bottom of the stairs, so I closed the box and headed out. Walking down the stairs, I heard Mom talking to Hercules as if they were old friends.

I approached her with hesitation, but she pulled me into a hug. "I'm sorry," she said, whispering in my ear. I shook my head and kissed her cheek. She let out a breath that sounded as if it carried an avalanche of emotions. "It'll take some time," she said. "You know that, right?"

I gave her a soft smile. This acknowledgment was a step in the right direction.

She dished up the two plates with eggs and toasted fresh bread, and I set the coffeepot on the table.

"Can we go to her grave?" she said as I sat down. I swallowed, surprised at how things were changing before my eyes. I didn't know if I'd imagined being here in the kitchen with her, sharing breakfast without throwing darts at each other.

"Let's wait until the next time I visit. Right now, I think we need to burn those letters."

Mom blinked in surprise.

"I know you've been reading them, and nothing good can come out of reading them over and over. It's the past. We already lived it. It's done."

She looked distressed. Still, without having touched my food, I got up, walked upstairs, and grabbed the box.

Mom met me in front of the fireplace. I paused before striking the match. Would destroying this evidence of my sister's affection for John be a betrayal, even after all these years? Mom had despised him because of his reputation for bragging about his sexual conquests. But Jenny had told me he wasn't like that. I didn't know what to think but remained loyal to Jenny.

I set fire to the rolled-up newspapers in the fireplace and then tossed the letters into the leaping flames.

"I am taking responsibility, Mom."

She winced a smile. She looked exhausted, and I felt the same way. Not going to the cemetery had been the right decision.

I would always be loyal to Jenny, but now I had to focus on my relationship with my mom. Otherwise, our bitterness would destroy us.

First Ending

Chapter 11

Wednesday, November 13

"IT HASN'T GROWN SINCE your last visit," Dr. Vera said. He pointed toward the images. They'd been taken a few minutes ago in another semidark room with a chatty technician who distracted me from my plight with pictures of fishing with his son. The man with a light blue outfit had captured the spot in the cornea with great accuracy after making me turn my head in all directions. The blotch was chestnut brown, like dried blood against the white globe. An anomaly that made me grimace every time I looked in the mirror.

"See, they're identical," the doctor continued. "It's good news, Andrew."

I gasped for air in the windowless room.

Several months ago, on a sunny day, nothing prepared me for the fact that I'd walk into this glass building and learn I might have cancer.

"Choroidal melanoma," Dr. Vera had said at that time, in a businesslike manner while striking his keyboard. The words had descended in front of me, aided by strings, and hung there until the next batch came out of his mouth in slow motion.

"We'll keep monitoring the spot to see if it grows. Some symptoms are loss of vision and floaters." He looked at me to see if I was following him. "The squiggly lines?"

I nodded.

"I've never heard of this type of thing happening to somebody my age," I managed to say.

"It's rare. It happens more often to people over fifty," Dr. Vera said.

My ears shut down after receiving that nifty piece of information. I'd heard the doctor's voice, but the words sounded distorted. The story I had to give to Bennett had come to mind as I sat, terrorized by my emotions. For weeks, finishing the story had been one of the only things keeping my spirit alive.

Now, I labored to breathe in the claustrophobic space. I couldn't yet grasp this new reality, the one where I was free from cancer.

"Andrew, can you hear me?" he said.

"Yeah, yeah, I'm fine."

He looked at me unconvinced. "Once something like this happens, we'll continue to monitor it every six months. And if everything is fine, once a year."

Leaving his office, I savored every step while I filled my lungs.

"Are you okay?" a nurse asked.

I realized I'd been standing in the hallway in a daze. For how long? I had no idea. I shook my head, and the nurse guided me to a sitting area.

"I'll bring you some water," she said.

"I thought my life was going to be over soon," I said when she returned with a paper cup. "Today, I got good news, but I'm still shaken."

She sat down beside me as I drank the water in one gulp. Then she extended her hand, and I squeezed it until I regained my composure.

As I walked outside, the sun struck me with all its might. I took another deep breath and grinned as the reality settled in further. I wanted to go out and celebrate. I opened my phone and scrolled down to Perico's name in my contact list. I even dialed his number.

"The number you are calling is out of service," the recording said. And he was beyond unreachable but now present only within my heart through memories. His departure was a true loss for me.

The thought of visiting Felicia tempted me. Then, I imagined trying to explain things to her. It would be tough if I was unwilling to get into all the details. I removed Bellatrix's card from my wallet. She at least knew part of the story—the most secretive one.

I made another call.

"Yes, the Specialist is working tonight," the voice said on the other end of the line. My mind ran to the massive red door, to the thought of tenderness without attachments.

"Please tell her Andrew will come over tonight."

"She'll be pleased," said the sweet voice on the other end.

ANDREW AND PROFESSOR LEVINE

Professor Levine was gazing at his computer when I knocked on his open door.

"May I come in?"

"You're glowing, Mr. Joseph."

"I've got good news, Professor," I said with a grin.

He glanced at his watch. "Come in. My next appointment is in two and a half hours, so we have plenty of time."

I bounced into the empty chair to the side of his desk. "The spot in my eye hasn't grown."

His eyes widened, and then he slammed his palms on the arms of his chair. "This calls for a celebration." He leaned down and retrieved an orange and an apple. "Take your pick."

I chose the bright red apple while he poured steaming dark fluid out of his thermos into an old mug that had been filled with pens a few seconds ago.

"You don't mind, do you?" he'd asked while blowing bursts of air into the mug before he poured in the coffee.

I shook my head and beamed. How could I mind anything after this news?

"Please don't tell anybody I offered you an apple with a cup of coffee," he said with a mischievous smile.

We raised our mugs in a toast, and I savored the hot, bitter liquid.

"This news changes everything, right, Professor? Now I can write one straightforward ending."

He took a slow sip. "I don't know about that. I think the alternate endings were always necessary, Andrew. I suggested it because—"

"Okay, okay," I said, interrupting him in my enthusiasm. "I'll include the good news in the first ending and see how Bennett reacts to it." I paused then, sobered a little by my thought. "But is that even necessary? Bennett, the character, wouldn't care about this news. Right?"

Professor Levine set down his thermos. "I'm glad you mentioned this. You argued earlier that everyone has some good within, or something to that effect." He continued in the peculiar low tone he used whenever he was about to weaken a student's most tenacious argument. "It's a crucial component of the story. Have you proven it yet? Some may refer to it as a thesis in progress."

There he was, the professor who poked holes into my story as if doing so were a pastime.

"Don't you think I reflect night and day trying to find some good in this character? And what if I can't? Is constant evil a flat character?"

He leaned back while fiddling with his suspenders.

"An interesting challenge, perhaps. How can a writer make a flat character, flat in his perversity, compelling? Not exactly a soup question, right, my friend?"

I smiled to myself. He'd never addressed me that way before. I picked up the stapler on his desk and opened it and closed it several times.

I'd been sincere with Perico. Though life and death had hung in the balance, I had truly believed the words that created so much heat between my loyal friend and me. I hadn't lied to save Bennett's life. I wanted to believe there was goodness in him.

Silence reigned in the room as I meditated on my theory. Bennett had sent me home early one day, saying, "You worked hard today. Go home. You deserve it." But that hadn't cost him anything. It wasn't his money, after all. No, it was more likely that he'd simply been trying to make himself look good.

The more I observed him, the more convinced I became that he spent most of his time thinking about how to hurt others for the sake of feeling powerful. That day in the basement hadn't been a spur-of-the-moment type of thing. I was sure about that. He'd planned and done it because he had the power to, believing there would be no repercussions. He'd looked so smug as he'd pulled up his zipper, singing a stupid little song.

Every time I remembered that moment, I wanted to strike—at midnight, at two in the morning, at four. Sometimes, I'd dream about killing him and would wake up drenched in sweat.

I took a deep breath.

"I still don't believe he's purely evil," I said. Yet my solar plexus tightened.

Professor Levine scratched his head and shifted his mouth slightly to the left in a grin of sorts.

"You want Bennett to prove my theory correct, don't you?" I said. "Perico would have words with you. He thought that two bullets would solve everything."

Professor Levine laughed through gleaming eyes.

"It's not about what I want, Andrew. Let the characters do what they want. You can't smother them. And since Bennett always reacts obnoxiously . . ." He shrugged. "I often ask students their thoughts on free will, and most swear they believe in it, but when I read their writing, their stiff characters tell me otherwise. See my point?"

"That's scary."

Professor Levine grabbed his chin.

"But back to the endings. Do you understand why you still need the alternate endings?"

"Honestly? No."

"It will give you room to explore the idea that people aren't always good or bad," he said. "And to test the idea of whether immoral actions always have consequences or not. Remember, Andrew, the character, interfered with the consequences twice. So, as far as Mr. Bennett knows, there are no penalties for evil."

I huffed. The professor had a point there. And it cut through me.

"Bennett chose a path," Professor Levine said. "That's irrefutable. The question is, Does one moral action—if you can find one—absolve past conduct if there's no genuine change?"

"It could, Professor." But I already sensed a deep conflict within my argument. A conflict I had been unaware of until now.

"See you in a few days, Andrew."

Chapter 12

PAGES FOR THE PROFESSOR

Wednesday, November 13

THE WHEELS DEVOURED THE asphalt on my way home, and as I climbed my steps, I heard Hercules scratching the door with such insistence that my hand became jittery and I dropped the keys. Once I stepped inside, he jumped around me for several minutes, perhaps feeling my own sense of relief. We both needed this occasion to celebrate after smelling ammonia for so long.

The evening sun bathed Perico's rubber tree, which had sprung a new leaf since his departure.

An hour later, while I was choosing my clothes for my rendezvous with Bellatrix, the doorbell purred; a quick *tap-tap* followed.

I grabbed my baseball bat from the living room closet but dropped it in surprise. Bellatrix stood on the porch. Her dark hair was draped over the left shoulder, and a purple flower pinned to it matched her violet-stained lips. Black leather suit. High heels.

The way she'd handled the dagger was still fresh in my mind. And lying on her blue silk sheets? That memory would stay there for a long time.

I let her in without a word, and her heels clicked on the wooden floor. "I hope that wasn't for me." She glanced at Hercules but didn't acknowledge him. Hercules took his distance as well but did not growl, yet his attentive eye caught her every move. I was curious as to why she had chosen the aloof attitude toward him.

"No, not at all," I said, trying to sound hospitable despite my shock. "I had an unpleasant visitor a few days ago. I called you at work and left a message that I was coming over."

"I figured I'd surprise you."

I cleared my throat. "I'm a little startled. I don't remember giving you my address."

"In my line of work, cunning is paramount. Do you mind if I take off my boots?" She didn't wait for an answer. Her toenails matched her lipstick and the flowers in her hair.

Hercules continued to observe her while she settled beside me on the L-shaped couch. He sniffed in her direction but didn't approach, which was unusual. Her scent was softer than the one she'd worn at the bordello—more alluring. But still, it had a lilac aroma, and it drew me near her.

Her gaze searched the room and stopped on the picture of her as a ten-year-old. Her expression betrayed nothing.

"I figured that my place of work wasn't the best setting to get to know each other," she said, looking away from the picture and back at me. "Too many interruptions. Don't you think?" She fluttered her eyelashes twice, enough to cause a struggle in me. She was desirable, but I wasn't sure if I could trust my instincts.

"Besides," she continued, "it's work. I wanted to see you outside that environment." Bellatrix let her finger slide over my cheek. "You strike me as a man who has no problems meeting women."

I cleared my throat again. "Hercules," I said in an admonishing tone to break her spell. "Come over here and say hello."

He got up and moved an inch closer but then lay down again, letting his snout rest over his front paws.

Bellatrix didn't look away from me. "Tell me about my father. What did a day with him look like?"

"You want the truth?" Every second was a surprise with her, and I felt I was under a magic charm when I was near her.

"Yes, I deal with hard truths every day, Andrew. And when it comes to him, I've had mixed emotions for a long time." With that, she glanced away.

"Anger spiced with loyalty and sprinkles of love."

She made a circular motion with her hand.

"Well, there was variety to our interactions," I said. "Sometimes our discussions got heated and bordered on the violent territory."

"What caused those discussions?"

"You already know. That's where the name Yoyo came from."

She looked at me with those glittering eyes and then spoke as if she hadn't perceived her effect on me. "Don't you think you've lost too much of your life thinking about that man?"

I inhaled to focus. "Right. I delivered Perico's eulogy before he passed away—in his hospital room while under the influence."

She raised her eyebrows in a rare show of emotion.

"You were drunk at the hospital?" she said, ignoring the last part of what I'd said.

"I was blowing off steam."

"I was ten years old in that picture," she said, glancing at the image on the coffee table again. More emotion crept into her expression, but she swallowed her minute outburst and stuffed her feelings into a paper bag.

"You don't strike me as being a drunkard, Andrew," she said, again changing tactics. "So, forgive me if I say it sounds a little off, delivering the eulogy before he's dead." Her demeanor was impossible to read. Even her tone was sweet.

"I'm not a drunkard, and you're right. It was surreal. I'd felt under duress for a long time. I was at the point of a breakdown—or maybe that's what happened."

Bellatrix gave me a subdued smile, then stood and went to the piano and sang a few lines. Her tone was beautiful, her pitch . . . Oh, I closed my eyes so nothing could distract me. Her sound filled every corner of the room. But she didn't hide the sadness nesting in her heart. The short cadence was so powerful that even Hercules perked up. Then she walked back to the couch and got close, facing me, eyes to eyes, lips to lips.

The doorbell put a stop to what I was hoping would happen next, since she broke all my barriers. Hercules barked while I stood to answer the door.

"Excuse me," I said to Bellatrix. Her smile I still remember.

When I opened the door, Felicia held up a bottle of wine. She wore jeans and a purple silk blouse. It was a purple evening. "Hi! Is this a good time?" Hercules sped to welcome her.

"Uh, it's fine," I said, but I was conflicted about having the two of them in my house. "Come in. I'm with my friend, Bellatrix, who stopped over, just like you."

I stumbled over how to introduce Felicia, but she picked up on it right away and rescued me seamlessly.

"I'm Felicia," she said, extending a hand to Bellatrix, who seemed amused. "His neighbor from across the street. He forgets," she said with a grin. "I take care of Hercules sometimes. I'm sorry for my intrusion. Are you his girlfriend, Bellatrix?"

"Oh, you don't pull any punches, girl. He wishes. No, I'm only visiting." She twirled her dark hair and patted the couch, indicating Felicia should sit. "Are you his girlfriend, Felicia?"

My neighbor shook her head and sat, after glancing at me.

"So, Andrew, how does it feel to have two beautiful women pay you a surprise visit?" Bellatrix asked.

"My knees are trembling," I said jokingly, trying not to let the truth of my words show.

Hercules stayed with them while I opened the wine and collected my thoughts.

After the initial surprise, I began to relax and enjoy their company, and I realized I was becoming a man again. They were such different women. Bellatrix's voice was deep and sensual, while Felicia's fizzled with energy. Bellatrix went directly for what she wanted. No hesitation. But Felicia was more elegant in her approach, yet daring as well. Perhaps they weren't all that different.

When I returned to the living room, Felicia had asked Bellatrix what she did for a living.

"Entertainment research," she said, without missing a beat. Both women gestured for me to sit between them. I swallowed and did so. Bellatrix placed her hand on my knee and leaned over me to get closer to Felicia. She was a master at giving signals.

"Is that how you two met?" Felicia asked. "It sounds mysterious, entertainment research."

I took a sip of my wine.

"We have a common business associate," Bellatrix said. "But enough about me, beautiful woman. You live across from him? I'm jealous."

They both looked at me.

"How long have you been alone, Andrew?" Felicia asked.

"My buddy and I got out of the monastery last week," I said with a chuckle, pointing at Hercules. The rascal barked twice.

"Someone is telling the truth," Felicia said, looking at Hercules.

I shrugged. "I stopped counting the years," I said, not knowing how much to reveal. I might have ended up telling Felicia everything if I'd been alone—she was warm and seemed trustworthy. But Bellatrix's presence reminded me of the stakes. I couldn't disclose everything to Felicia without putting her in danger.

Felicia nodded and took a sip of her drink. "Why did you stop counting?" Then, she gestured to the picture of Bellatrix. "Who's that girl? There's something magnetic about her."

"I'd been living in a fog because of trauma and guilt, where keeping count felt pointless." I looked to Bellatrix for help with the other question, unsure how much to reveal.

"It's a picture of me when I was ten," Bellatrix said.

Felicia frowned a little. "So, you two have known each other your whole lives?"

"Not that long. The picture came into Andrew's possession through my father," Bellatrix said, giving me a tender stare.

"I've seen it before but didn't want to pry," Felicia said. "My condolences, Bellatrix."

Bellatrix acknowledged her words with a nod. "I understand you called the ambulance for my father?"

Felicia nodded, and rubbed her right cheek nervously.

The three of us chitchatted until the wine was gone. Bellatrix was the first to stand. "It's late. I'll escort Felicia to her house—to protect her from you." She twisted her lips playfully and left the purple flower on my coffee table. Felicia noticed but didn't comment.

When they were gone, Hercules sniffed the spot where Bellatrix's naked feet had been.

My senses were overwhelmed, and my body was electrified with their presence. Enough had occurred in one night. Mom wouldn't believe it—so I went to sleep happy. It was a form of healing, enjoying being a man again.

Chapter 13

Thursday, November 14

"**Zemira, this is Yoyo**, otherwise known as Andrew," Bennett said, as the three of us stood in his office. "Yoyo will train you today. You're on your own tomorrow."

My eyes widened, and my heart sank.

Bennett rubbed the scar below his eye to the point where it became uncomfortable to watch.

"Zemira's taking Perico's spot," he said to me, still rubbing his scar. "Sorry for not giving you a heads-up, Yoyo." A lascivious smile made its way onto Bennett's face as he scanned Zemira's body from top to bottom.

The young woman nodded at my mechanical greeting and shook my hand. Her grip had power.

"Zemira will do Perico's floors," he said, continuing to look at her as though she were on display in a store window. "Her uniform isn't here yet, but I want her to start right away. Teach her how to use the buffing machine. Enjoy the day," Bennett said, practically singing the last sentence.

I thought of the song he'd sung in the basement and felt these volcanic emotions within. No one was safe from his sexual innuendos. But what disturbed me more was the fact that Perico's replacement was finally here. He should have outlasted Bennett.

"Don't forget to sign in, Yoyo."

As I bent to do so, my attention was caught by the words *Industrial accident* written beside Chuchoka's name. I could feel Bennett's eyes on me. I saw the tremor in my hand as I signed my name.

Just then, a middle-aged man entered the office. In his wake was a garlicky odor with a hard-liquor base. Zemira scrunched up her nose. I wasn't sure why, but a chill traveled down my back. The boss treated him with unusual politeness—strange for a newcomer. Terry Scarpo was the new name on the sign-in sheet. And though introducing new people to the other workers was customary, Bennett waved us away.

We walked to the elevator in silence, but as soon as the doors closed, Zemira said, "Our friend Bellatrix sent me to keep an eye on things."

I blinked, startled. Keep an eye on things? Was this part of the business of axing Bennett? Or was Bellatrix genuinely concerned about me?

"That's nice, but what would you do if that animal attacked you? No offense, but could you handle a tall guy like Bennett—maybe right here in this elevator?" I asked Zemira, who looked eerily similar to Bellatrix but about ten years younger.

"This." She pressed the red Stop button, and the car came to a shuddering halt. The alarm rang. From her back pocket, she removed a retractable knife and shoved it against my genitals while throwing me to the wall with her left forearm pressed against my neck.

She was strong in her compact frame. Bellatrix had trained her, no doubt. There was no wasted motion.

"Do you want me to flick the knife's switch and show you what I can do?" she said with fierce eyes while her voice remained cuddly and a sweet smile adorned her face.

"No, no," I blurted. "There's no need," I said. "You convinced me." She backed away and placed the knife in her pocket. I exhaled. "I'm glad I don't have to worry about you getting—" I cleared my throat. "But the bastard knocked me out from behind."

I heard my words, which sounded like an attempt to regain my manhood. "Anyway, I'm glad this training session is going so well," I said, fixing my shirt. "I can tell you're a quick learner."

The alarm still rang loud and shrill.

"Bellatrix told me to show you love," Zemira said. "We all express it in different ways."

Through the metal doors, a man's muffled voice rang. "Is everything okay in there?"

"Please help us, please! We're stuck," Zemira said with the flair of an actress. Then she turned toward me and said quietly, "Bellatrix couldn't be here because Bennett has seen her on Beacon Street." She gave me a quick peck on the lips. "Friends?"

I'd gone from a knife to my crotch to a kiss on my lips in mere moments. My head spun.

Zemira flipped the red emergency switch that stopped the elevator, and we jolted into motion again.

As we buffered Perico's floors, his departure became real for me in a whole new way. The absence of that rumbling voice—it crushed me. It was cruel, my having to train Perico's replacement. It was as if Bennett had planned it that way.

I stopped. Of course he had.

Zemira looked at me. "Are you thinking about your friend who worked on these floors?"

"You're perceptive."

"It was Bellatrix's idea. She knows you took care of her father. It's her way of saying thank you."

With that, I crumpled to the floor and leaned against the wall, more confused than ever. I needed clarity in my life. But perhaps Bellatrix's actions weren't so confusing, and there was genuine gratitude behind them. I never expected her to care about me in such a tangible fashion, especially after coming to her with a weird story and a dagger.

Zemira stopped buffing and put the spray bottle on the floor. Sitting beside me, she grabbed my hand. "I know you're in pain."

When lunchtime came, I asked Zemira if she wanted to see where Perico and I had hung out. We sat on the ledge, and I split my ham sandwich with her. No rowers glided over the Charles River, and the megaphone reigned in silence.

"So, did you and Bellatrix work together over at Beacon Street?" I asked Zemira, breaking the momentary quietness.

She just smiled.

"What are you allowed to say?"

"Not much. Only that you should feel reassured about Bellatrix being your friend and that your enemies should dread you."

The words were nice, no doubt. But Bennett had hurt me in the past despite Perico's good intentions. I needed to be able to protect myself.

We returned to work, and Zemira spoke only when spoken to. It was better that way. I had to focus on drafting the rest of the story in my head. The sooner I wrote it, the sooner Filomena could read it to the bony man downstairs.

That evening, the campus sizzled with life between classes. When the dark clock on Commonwealth Avenue struck the hour, the thick bronze doors spewed students until the concrete walkways were a multitude of chattering colors. Chaos ensued until the next class began. Then the walkways became deserted. Outside, occasionally, the green train cars glided over the iron tracks—the rails that separated the opposite sides of Commonwealth Avenue across the bronze doors.

On my way out of class, I saw Filomena atop the steps overlooking the avenue. I approached and touched her shoulder.

She startled a little, then smiled. "Hi. How's the story coming along? I haven't heard from you, Yoyo. I didn't know if you still wanted me to read it?"

"Oh yes, you're a critical reader in this project," I said with a humorless chuckle.

Filomena gave me a quizzical look. I wanted to tell her she was a critical element in saving her father's life.

"Can you tell me a little more about it?" she said.

"Healing. It's about healing, but it's also about a person whose life is at stake. So I need to make sure the narrative is sharp."

"Why me?"

I tried to appear nonchalant. "You gave me the impression you were open-minded. If you're open-minded and impartial, I can trust your feedback. I'll give you a questionnaire. Take my number so I can get the story to you if something happens."

"If something happens?" She frowned. "You're a mysterious man, Andrew."

At that moment, I saw Bennett looking at us from across the street, next to the convenience store, beyond the black bars dividing the trolley tracks. He didn't look pleased.

"There's Dad," she said, waving at him.

A trolley went by, and when it had passed, Bennett was gone. A knot formed in my stomach.

"Starting Monday, are you comfortable continuing on your own, Zemira?" Bennett asked the next morning in his office.

"Yes, I think I can manage. Right, Andrew?" She gave me an innocent smile and patted me on the back.

"Oh, yeah, she can handle herself. For sure, Mr. Bennett. She's a natural with the buffer." It had been a long time since I addressed him as mister. To me, the word *mister* implied respect.

Bennett gave Zemira a forced smile and once again avoided looking at me. Earlier that morning, we'd encountered each other in the hall, and he hadn't said a word about seeing me with Filomena.

Odd.

In fact, he hadn't looked me in the eye for a couple of days.

"You look worried," Zemira said once we were in the elevator.

"It's nothing. It's just that Bennett saw me talking to his daughter yesterday, and he'd warned me not to. He hasn't said anything about it to me today. He usually cannot hold his anger."

Her eyes narrowed. "Bellatrix told me to watch you closely for your protection. She mentioned your home has a basement." She looked at me pointedly. "She thinks Bennett will strike again."

"Bennett attacked me at work, Zemira," I snapped, then softened my tone. "I mean, I worry that he will attack me again. That's why I try not to be alone with him. But my place? I don't know. It's hard to believe. Don't you think?"

"Okay, I offered," she said with a shrug. "But I think you're afraid of inviting me to your place—because your neighbor might see me. The pretty one with the red sports car."

I scoffed. "I'm not afraid. Who's this talking anyway, you or Bellatrix? And it's not my fault she's pretty." My ears burned.

After work, Zemira and I headed to the parking lot together. She unlocked a black sedan with tinted glass and no hubcaps, then grabbed a business card from her glove compartment.

"It's my cell number," she said, handing it to me. "I wouldn't strike in the same place twice if I were Bennett."

I drove home feeling unsettled. Once inside, I moved through the entire house and checked every window, with Hercules trailing. There were two small ground-level windows, which had metal canopies to protect them from the elements. These windows had always made me feel a little exposed. I mean, some thief could use them to break into the house.

A sensation in my chest directed me to open the front door, and to my surprise, I saw Zemira's black sedan cruising by. She made a U-turn and parked at the top of the hill, facing my house. I also noticed that Felicia's car wasn't in her driveway.

When I realized Zemira had no intention of coming in, I closed the door and went to the rear entrance to let Hercules out into the fenced backyard. Usually, I'd prepare coffee while he did his business in the half-moon-shaped patch of grass. This time, I stayed outside with him. I gazed at the rosebushes I'd planted around the fence. For some reason, one I couldn't explain, I felt this strange sensation in my chest, which had never failed to warn me when something was about to happen. There was a slight chill in the air, and the reddish and gray clouds siphoned the last vestiges of light on the horizon.

When Hercules was done, we went back inside, and I grabbed the blue velvet bag from the nightstand in Perico's old bedroom, facing the backyard. I took out the bullets and tossed them on the bedspread. Then I raised the gun, pointed it at the window, and pulled the trigger. The click sounded as I'd imagined. I trembled while I imagined the recoil.

Tossing the weapon on the comforter, I stepped back and hit the wall. I took a few deep breaths. Then I fumbled the bullets back into their chambers. My hand struck the cylinder. There was something musical in that whirring sound. I was bewitched in the presence of an instrument of death.

It was the first time that I'd prepared for a looming danger in such a methodical fashion.

Seemingly feeling my mood, Hercules scratched at my leg. I set down the gun, picked him up, and held him close, just as I had when he was a puppy. I'd brought him home inside my leather jacket like a burrito stuck to my heart. We bonded right away.

As a last precaution, I sent Bellatrix a text.

Can you check Terry Scarpo with your contacts? Bennett looks very close to him at work. Zemira is outside in her car.

Invite her in, she replied. *Outside, she's of no help to you.*

When Zemira entered, Hercules sniffed her and wagged his tail. She took her time with him, and he showed her extreme affection in response. The rascal even extended himself on the wooden floor so she could rub his belly. She knelt and kissed his stomach before rubbing noses with him, acting as if there was no impending danger.

"Hercules," I said with an admonishing tone. "She has business to take care of."

But the two of them ignored me. My phone vibrated in my pocket.

Scarpo got out of a Mexican jail a couple of months ago. Lock everything. I'm on my way.

Chapter 14

Thursday, November 14

PERICO'S OLD .38 LAY next to my right hand, and Hercules rested at my feet. Sitting on the floor in the dining room, next to the rubber tree, I remembered when I first settled in the place and had no furniture. I'd sat against the wall and watched the flashes of headlights going up and down the street.

Zemira had gone into the basement, leaving the door to the kitchen ajar. She had a direct view of the part of the hallway that led to the bedroom.

I had turned off all the lights, but the streetlight in front of the house created a shadowy illumination in the room. For a moment, I was taken back to the night at the arboretum. Instinctively, I touched my neck.

The house moaned as if in labor. The crickets sang, and I heard the furnace start. Warm air flowed through the register, and then there was a soft *tap-tap* on the front door.

My heart raced, so I stood and walked barefoot to the door. "Bellatrix?" I said softly.

"Yes, it's me," she said, and I let her in. "Zemira?" she said, moving through the house. I showed her the spot where I had barricaded in the dining room, next to the rubber tree, with a line of sight to the front door.

"I'm here," Zemira called softly.

Bellatrix moved to the kitchen door and opened it farther. "I'll ensure Scarpo doesn't come through this way. Scarpo has a proclivity for violence. So, if you have the chance . . ." she said to Zemira.

"Got it, sis."

Sis?

When Bellatrix sat down next to me, I looked at her and asked with my eyes.

"Yes. Sis. Zemira was born several months after Dad got arrested. He never met her. Mom hid the pregnancy from him, but I always observed him from a distance." She paused. "Mom never recovered from postpartum depression, and from then on, it was all downhill. She was kept in a place that looked like a hospital. Zemira and I got separated and didn't see each other for a long time. She had better luck with her adoptive parents. One day, I met a character called Chuchoka outside our apartment building, and he told me he was Dad's friend."

"Our Chuchoka?"

She nodded. "'I'll occasionally ask you about him,' I told him. 'I'll kill you if you tell him where to find me, though.' He looked into my eyes to see if I could kill someone. He kept quiet."

"Chuchoka doesn't scare easily," I said.

"The bastard told me he had seen my sister in the neighborhood. So, I visited from time to time—never at her place. Zemira would make an excuse to go to the store. Whenever she wanted to see me, she'd leave a golden scarf by the window. I went by her house every day."

"Does Zemira work on Beacon Street?"

"No, she'll never do that, but she freelances with me when I need her on this other gig. I do the dirty work, but she's a backup. It feels good to have her close to me."

Bellatrix took a .22 from her purse and screwed a silencer on it before letting it rest on the floor. Then she removed the dagger. Another dreadful instrument of death. But the desire to kill wasn't in the weapons. It came from us. From Bellatrix and me. I reached for the handle and lifted the blade close to my nose.

"Do you feel attracted to it?" I asked.

"I do, but not like you. It's simply a tool for me. There's still innocence in you."

"I think we're overreacting."

"Better to overreact than leave ourselves at the mercy of Scarpo and Bennett. They won't take any pity on you. You still don't realize who you're dealing with."

Her pragmatic words sounded so final and left me with a strange sensation in my gut—tight, real tight. I thought of the time I put too much pepper on the meat loaf my mom had made. Mom had spent the whole morning making it and abhorred when Jenny and I left anything on our plates. I had to force myself to eat it.

"What about Zemira?" I asked.

"What about her?"

"Tell her to take care of herself," I said. "I don't want to train somebody else at work. She handles the buffer like a pro." I looked into Bellatrix's interrogating eyes. "She also has a flair for creating lasting impressions. She pulled a knife on me and placed it right there," I said, pointing between my legs.

She laughed quietly. "Sounds like my little sis. She's fine. She'll stay in the basement until the song starts."

"The song?"

"Yeah. *Pow, pow.* Do you know how to fire a gun?"

"No, but I imagine all I have to do is point and squeeze the trigger." I held up one hand and mimed firing a shot.

Bellatrix shook her head and frowned her lips. "Since it's your first time, hold it with both hands," she said, imitating the recoil.

"Why are you going through all this trouble for me?"

"I've known about you for a while," she said, gazing straight ahead. "Like I said, I tracked my dad over the years. I knew what was going on, that you took him in at the end."

We fell into a comfortable silence.

Then Bellatrix said softly, "I would have liked to have drinks without any interruptions. Though I liked your friend Felicia. She's pretty."

I looked at her. It seemed as if she was giving me her blessing to go in that direction if I wanted to. But in this moment, that wasn't at all what I wanted. I moved closer. Bellatrix let the gun rest on the floor and pulled me in for a long, soft kiss.

That's when I heard the unmistakable sound of glass breaking. Hercules growled and stood, looking toward Perico's old bedroom.

"Always interrupted," Bellatrix said. She tapped the floor twice with the silencer to alert Zemira and then lifted her weapons, the gun in her right hand and the dagger in her left. She crawled toward the living room. Suddenly, Hercules bolted to the rear bedroom. I tried to grab him, but he squeezed through my hands. Before I could get to him, he gave a sudden yelp.

I plunged into the shadows. The scents of liquor and garlic filled the hallway. At the sound of a muffled *pop-pop!* I dropped to the floor. A powdery odor engulfed me. I was vaguely aware of a burning sensation, and it was difficult to breathe.

I heard a groan and the sound of someone falling heavily.

Lights came on.

Something skittered across the floor.

A gun cocked.

"No. Put it away. That's why I hit him on the head. He can't talk if he's dead," Bellatrix said sternly.

"Right, like he's going to confess, sis."

"A little persuasion, a little love. That's all a man needs to open up."

I opened my eyes to see Bellatrix at my left side, holding some towels. "Press these against your side."

"And my baby?"

"I am here," Zemira said aloud.

"No, Hercules."

"He's alive," Zemira said.

"Just knocked out," Bellatrix added. "Zemira. Get over here." Bellatrix grabbed another towel once she learned one of Scarpo's shots had grazed my forearm.

"I'll take Hercules to the vet," Zemira said.

Bellatrix ripped a strip off a towel and tied Scarpo's hands behind his back. Then she stuffed all the weapons in a duffel bag except Scarpo's .22.

Finally, she grabbed my phone. "I want to report a break-in at Nine Gladeside Avenue, Mattapan. An intruder shot my boyfriend. He needs an ambulance. Please hurry. The intruder, he's tied."

I'd never heard apprehension in Bellatrix's voice before.

"Stay awake, Andrew," she shouted.

Chapter 15

Saturday, November 16

BELLATRIX'S RIGHT HAND RESTED over the armchair in an alert slumber, but when I coughed, she lifted her baseball cap and stared at me while the left hand dozed faithfully inside her purse.

A young nurse entered the room and adjusted the drip, setting the trigger near my fingers. The memory of the gunpowder stung my nostrils. It was alluring and repugnant. I felt the weapon's short thunder as stinging bees in my flesh. My body jolted.

"Hercules?" I said in desperation, speaking for the first time since the incident.

"He's at the vet," Bellatrix said, uncrossing her legs and then recrossing them with the other leg on top. Her boots were next to the chair. "He suffered a nasty blow to the head, but he'll make it."

"What happened to me?"

"The bullets grazed your side and forearm. It's a good thing Scarpo was a bad shooter," Bellatrix said with a faint smile.

It all felt like a bad dream. And all I wanted was to get up and go to Hercules. Bellatrix placed her hand over mine until I started breathing in a more relaxed manner. "And Scarpo?" I asked.

"He's in police custody. I knocked him out with the butt of the dagger. Too bad it wasn't Bennett." I felt relieved nobody was killed at home. But my mind couldn't process much right now. The news about Hercules reduced my anxiety, even though he had been hurt.

Sometime later, the doctor came to check on me. "Your prognosis is excellent, Andrew. Superficial wounds. They'll sting, but you'll heal quickly. We'll take good care of him, Mrs. Joseph. It's a good thing you were with him. Otherwise, he might have lost too much blood." He looked back at me. "You'll spend the night here, and tomorrow morning, we'll see. Maybe we'll move you to a room."

"Mrs. Joseph?" I said to Bellatrix after the doctor left. I couldn't muster the energy to laugh. "Weren't you my girlfriend a brief time ago?"

"It was my way into the ICU," she said with a shrug. "I knew you wouldn't mind. And don't worry about work. I left a message for Bennett saying that somebody tried to murder you in your own home. I'm sure it shook him to his glass eye. The police are going to stop by and ask you some questions. They know I was there, but they don't know about Zemira. I want to keep her out of this."

I didn't want Zemira to be questioned by the police, either. She didn't deserve that. Already, too many people had been hurt trying to help me. "I understand, dear. I'm tired, Mrs. Joseph."

"Sleep. I'll be here."

When I woke up the next morning, Bellatrix was still with me, and a nurse was checking my wounds and vital signs. Soon after, the doctor allowed the transfer out of the ICU. The nurse rolled me to a room on the fifth floor. It had a view of the South Shore.

Once I was settled, Bellatrix walked to the window and looked outside. "I'm afraid our friend Mr. Bennett won't get to read your story." The glass was covered with water lines from the recent rain.

I exhaled. Bennett's actions had sent all my intentions reeling, which confused me even more in this state.

"The idea of Bennett changing . . ." Bellatrix said with a certain displeasure, turning toward me. "Look," she said more gently, "he made his choice before reading your story. He escalated the situation by sending an assassin to your home. I'd say he broke the contract. Sure, it was a contract he wasn't aware of, but you negotiated for him in good faith."

"I can't believe he sent somebody to the house." It was all I could say.

"Have you finished it?" Bellatrix asked.

"I was close. And then this." I coughed and gestured to the room with my hand. "I suppose all this will make its way onto the page now." I groaned at the realization that I was going to have to finish it with one hand.

Bellatrix took off her baseball cap and fluffed up her hair. "Andrew, why go through the trouble now?"

"I'm writing it to heal. That's all that matters now. Please," I said, making one last attempt, "don't do anything rash."

This time, she exhaled. "Okay, my dear. But I'll tell you one thing—now I understand why Dad was so angry with you."

"It's always good to understand," I said weakly.

"And if Scarpo talks, all bets are off, and it's bye-bye, Bennett."

I tried to think about the ramifications, but the IV drip felt too good. I dozed off, and when I woke again, Felicia stood beside me, umbrella in hand.

"Bellatrix told me you were here. She went to go get your mother."

"I don't want to cause you trouble," I said, suddenly overwhelmed. But the prospect of Mom seeing me like this made me uncomfortable. Bellatrix could handle herself with Mom, so that wasn't a problem. In a few hours, Mom would see two women around me. And I feared her mouth. She didn't know how to keep her cool.

I had gone across the street and asked a perfect stranger to help me with Hercules, and now here she was at the hospital, ready to care for me.

"I have to make sure Hercules has a father," she said with a sympathetic smile.

Detectives Rosa Ramos and John Placid arrived in the mid-afternoon. I was still under the influence of the sedatives.

They were dressed in suit jackets and dark pants. They had a no-nonsense type of attitude. Felicia stayed by the window, sensing the tension.

After explaining that my attacker was behind bars, the detectives told me they had a few routine questions for me. I cringed. There was nothing routine about this situation.

"Do you know this man?" Detective Ramos held up a mug shot. "He's an American but was in Tijuana for a while."

"Yes, he's the new guy at work. Terry Scarpo."

"Did you cross him?" she asked, with a stony face.

"Not that I'm aware of. I don't know him, but Bennett, my boss, seems to know him well."

"What do you mean?" The detective's tone was polite but firm. Biting even.

"I've never exchanged a word with the guy, but Scarpo and Bennett seem to be friendly with each other." I paused, unsure how much to reveal. Bennett behind bars sounded like a good idea. But putting him there would require getting into what he'd done to me. And I had no desire to reveal that, detective or not. "Bennett's not exactly a social butterfly," I said finally.

"Do you get along with your boss?"

"I'm tired and hurting," I said, exhausted by the inquiry.

The detectives exchanged a glance.

"Yes, of course," said Detective Ramos. "I think we've got enough for now. Get well, Mr. Joseph."

The two walked toward the door, but before leaving, they turned around. "Nobody has seen Mr. Bennett," Detective Ramos said. "It's strange for your boss to disappear. We'll leave an officer outside as a precaution in case Scarpo had an accomplice."

"Great. Thank you for looking out for me," I said.

"Why would somebody want to kill you, Mr. Joseph?" Detective Placid asked, speaking for the first time. His voice was throaty. "What are we missing? We're missing something." He took a step back toward the bed. "And your friend. Bellatrix. It would be challenging to disarm a criminal like Scarpo. Who's she?"

Knowing where he wanted me to go, I remained silent. To hell with these detectives for making me feel guilty. I was innocent.

The next day, I woke up feeling confused. Then Felicia was there by my bed. "Do you need me?"

"Yes, I do." I squeezed her hand.

The hours passed and the room got dark. Felicia got up to contemplate the expanse of trees and rooftops. There was a beautiful glow on the horizon. A thick line of yellow and orange fused with each other, impossible to separate.

"I've been thinking," she said. "It would be good for you to stay at my house with Hercules until you recover."

"That's kind of you. But you're going out of your way for me. Why?"

"Do I need to say it?"

I surrendered with a smile. Having her close to me with her peaceful aura made me glad I had crossed the street asking for help. There was no doubt she had feelings for me, and I began to enjoy being loved and my own budding feelings of love for her.

In the morning, the detectives returned for a quick visit while Felicia was still with me.

"We questioned Scarpo, and he gave up Bennett," Detective Ramos said. "There's a warrant out for his arrest."

"Scarpo confessed?" I asked, unable to hide my surprise.

"Yes, after your friend Bellatrix visited him."

"That must have been quite the conversation."

"We feel the same way," Detective Placid said. "We have a signed confession saying that Bennett sent Terry Scarpo to your house to murder you. The question is, Why, Mr. Joseph? It's unusual for a guy with such a rap sheet to confess."

"I'm not sure I can help you there," I said, but I knew my time was up. The detective wasn't going to let this go until I gave him something. And I didn't want to give him Bellatrix. Still, I wished Felicia hadn't been in the room.

"Bennett raped me at work," I said evenly. For once my voice didn't break as I said the words.

But I pressed the call button. The nurse walked in and sensed the mood in the room. "That's enough for today," she said with full authority to the detectives.

"If there weren't any witnesses," Detective Placid said, ignoring her, "then it's he said, you said. But justice tends to come one way or the other, Mr. Joseph. If we can charge him with that crime, we'll do it."

After they left, I looked at Felicia. She took my hand and squeezed it.

"Do you understand now why I've been distant?"

"Yes, I do. My offer still stands."

Chapter 16

Tuesday, November 19

That afternoon, Bellatrix returned to the hospital with my mom, who carried a light blue purse and wore a blue hat. Mom always wore something blue, no matter the occasion, and Jenny teased her about it. She'd never explained to us the obsession with the color, though.

The one time I'd asked her about it, in that big kitchen of the Greenfield house, she'd said, "Son, a mother needs to keep a few things to herself." With that, she tossed her blue apron on the kitchen table and opened the French doors overlooking the half moon of trees in the backyard, barren because of the season. The teakettle whistled like a freight train while she dabbed her eyes with her blue hankie.

Now, here she was with Bellatrix, who was encouraging her to approach me. She embraced me, which was strange.

When she pulled away, Mom introduced herself to Felicia, and they chatted for a few minutes. "Oh, my dear, you really listen to me," Mom said at one point. "It's refreshing," she added, glancing at me—like a slight reproach.

Bellatrix looked down, and so did Felicia. The heat in the room became stifling.

"Why don't we get some warm drinks in the cafeteria, Mrs. Joseph?" Felicia said with a smile, adjusting her own blue scarf, which was gorgeous against her white dress. "You must be tired from the trip."

But Mom put her purse and hat on the bed and gazed at me with nurturing eyes. My insides rumbled. I thought of the time when I drove too fast down the road in Greenfield, and Jenny told me to hit the brakes. "Let's take this dirt road and see where it goes!" I'd taken a ninety-degree turn sharply. I felt a void in my stomach.

"I'll be staying with Felicia while I recover," I told Mom to break the silence that was becoming awkward for me and, I suppose, for Bellatrix as well.

Mom nodded with a look of approval. "I think you're in excellent hands." Dimples of joy formed in her cheeks as she reached out and felt the texture of Felicia's scarf. Then she focused her attention on me once more. "I heard the police caught the intruder."

"Yeah, well, they caught the guy who pulled the trigger, but the person behind the attempt is still out there."

Her face grew pale. "So that's why there's a police officer outside your door. I told you—your place is at home."

"We've talked about this, Mom."

"Yes. Anyway. We have so much to discuss."

"But now is not the time, Mom," I said, too tired to hide my impatience. "I'll come to visit you soon."

Thankfully, Mom left it at that and agreed to join Felicia for a drink in the cafeteria. Once they'd left, I turned toward the window where Bellatrix stood.

"The police were here. What did you say to Scarpo?" I said, trying to hide how nervous I felt. I knew Bellatrix was a pro, but I also recognized she had the capacity to make dangerous decisions. And Scarpo didn't seem the type to offer up a confession.

"Oh, I already forgot," Bellatrix said, glancing at her long dark nails. "You don't have to worry about details like that." She looked at me. "Hercules is recovering well," she said with a cheerful tone. "Zemira will pick him up tomorrow and take him to Felicia's house."

"You saved my life, Bellatrix."

Her straight hair hung to her waist and gleamed in the rays of sun filtering into the room.

"My dad would have done the same thing. Don't you think?"

"Yes, he would have. What did you say to Scarpo?"

A smile made its way onto her face.

"You want to know the actual words?"

"It would help."

"'My tentacles can reach behind the prison walls.'" She smirked. "That's what I whispered in the interrogation room. I also told him he was alive because I'd chosen not to terminate his stinky self." She walked a little closer to my bed. "I also paid Mr. Bennett a visit. I had somebody tag him so I could stay up to date on his whereabouts."

I blinked. "You've been busy. The detectives said they hadn't located Bennett."

"Doesn't surprise me," she said, scoffing. "I seduced Bennett into talking with me after my visit to Scarpo. 'Somewhere private,'" she said, making air quotes. "In a dingy room by the river, to be precise. I slipped a little something into his drink, and it made him quite talkative."

My eyes flew open. Just how lethal she was—I realized I was ill-prepared for dealing with this unknown dimension of hers.

"Yeah," she continued, "he felt sure he'd escaped repercussions. Too bad he trusted Scarpo." She paused and looked at me cautiously. "Do you want to know what he said to me?"

My heart raced, but I couldn't stop my mouth from saying yes. Even if what she had to say was horrible. I'd run through many scenarios, explanations, and justifications to rationalize the insanity of saving somebody like Bennett. I needed the truth.

Bellatrix held my gaze. "Bennett said, 'Andrew brought it on himself. He's weak. Pathetic.'"

There it was. It was strange to hear it, but it sounded like something he'd say. Yet Bennett didn't know that I had fought for him so he could continue to breathe.

"But what he said about his boss was quite interesting," Bellatrix said. "He told me that Mr. Diedra authorized him to mistreat you as he saw fit because you went against the department and defended your colleague in court."

"Maybe this changes things," I said with a sigh. "If Diedra is ultimately at fault."

"You can't eliminate all the devils at once. In this situation, you have to choose." Bellatrix gave a little chuckle before she spoke again. "Bennett started raging, saying, 'Who does Andrew think he is, believing he has the power to fight us.'

"Then I stabbed the chair right between his legs. I stabbed it eleven times. He screamed like—"

"I'm glad you didn't kill him!" I blurted.

"I gave you my word, didn't I?"

"He really said all of that to you?"

"Nothing like a little love, persuasion, and spiked coffee," she said, and laughed hard.

She would never cease to surprise me. "I'm not sure I approve of your method, but thank you. I'll never be able to repay you."

"Hey," she said with a shrug, "I restrained myself from killing your dear Mr. Bennett. What else do you want from me? Anyway, I told him, 'I'm sure putting a couple of bullets in Andrew wasn't part of the "mistreatment allowance" your boss gave you. You took it too far, Bennett.'"

That was putting it mildly, I thought.

"Anyway, I must go. I'd thought bringing your mom to the hospital would be positive. Oh, by the way, I anonymously gave the police the location of where Bennett is. Maybe take the story to his cell in jail," she said sarcastically, and added, "Perhaps he'll become a monk after he reads it."

Bellatrix blew me a kiss and disappeared before I could respond, leaving me to sort through my feelings on my own.

Chapter 17

Monday, November 25

BELLATRIX ALL BUT VANISHED in the days that followed. I'd texted her only once, the day I left the hospital, asking if she was going to stop by Felicia's to visit. And all day, I'd been glued to my phone, waiting for a reply. When the week came to an end, I had to concede the truth—she wanted distance. The kiss was still strong in my mind.

Hercules was in good spirits but limped, favoring his front left leg. He meandered between his food dish and the guest room at Felicia's house. On Monday morning, having spent the weekend at Felicia's house, I decided to move back to my place. I needed to get back to some semblance of normality.

"Don't you think it's too soon?" Felicia said.

"I'm just across the street," I reminded her with an affectionate grin.

Felicia and I were getting closer, and she brought joy to my life. She took me as I was. She was emotionally healthy, for sure, and an only child. Both her parents were alive. After attending university, Felicia got a good-paying job at an insurance company and climbed to executive status. Her upbeat personality attracted me, but she also had a quiet, contemplative, even spiritual side. And with Bellatrix keeping her distance, I felt free to explore my feelings for her.

In doing so, I observed how she lived, more than what she said. She was a woman who showed love through her actions. She tended to my wounds and left chocolates on the counter. And I'd never seen Hercules happier. I found myself falling for her as well.

"I need to put my house in order," I said. "You understand, right?" I hugged her, and her body felt right against mine. "Your life is already in order."

"All right, but don't overdo it. I'll be checking on you."

As I walked across the street, aided by Perico's old walking stick, Hercules limped beside me, and I chuckled at the thought of what Perico might say if he could see me.

A chill ran down my spine. I'd probably never feel totally comfortable here again. I might even have to move.

The hallway was stained with my blood, once red, but now a darkish brown. And the rubber tree's leaves were limp for lack of water.

In Perico's old bedroom, facing the backyard where I sat contemplating the birds, the floor was littered with shattered glass, and a piece of plywood covered the broken pane. Wanting to keep busy, I retrieved some tools from the basement and took the frame off its track so I could replace the windowpane. At my workbench, I removed the last vestiges of jagged glass and smoothed the track. A sense of peace came over me as I secured chunks of putty to the frame and glass. The previous owner had left behind several extra windowpanes. I'd never imagined they'd come in handy. The house regained its warmth after the repair, but I was still cold.

Healing might never fully arrive, but I finally knew how to conclude the first ending. I placed the broken pieces in a cardboard box and set them outside by the side door, ready for garbage day on Wednesday.

On Friday, the campus was empty. Filomena's back rested against the library building next to the Charles River with its magnificent dark granite walls. She had responded to my text: *I'm doing some research. I'll be right outside.*

"Here's the manuscript and a questionnaire, as promised," I said when she came out. I paused before handing it over. "You still give your dad books to read, right?"

"Yes," Filomena said, but she seemed more interested in my injury than the manuscript. "What happened to you?"

"A little accident."

She covered her mouth.

"I'm getting better. Anyway, I'd love for you to give this one to your dad. See if he likes it. I actually dedicated it to him."

Filomena flipped to the dedication page and read it aloud: *"For Mr. Bennett. This story wouldn't have been possible without your silent encouragement."*

Filomena looked at me with a question in her eyes, but I just thanked her for her time and turned to walk away.

"I haven't seen him for a few days," she said.

"Oh," I said, glancing back. "Well, whenever you see him." Walking away felt like I had left an enormous coat loaded with stones in its pockets on the ground. The breeze from the river refreshed me.

Felicia waited for me in the parking lot. At my insistence, she drove us to the baseball field on Jamaicaway and parked the car. There was no one practicing this time.

I decided to tell everything to Felicia, so there wouldn't be any secrets between us. "I put up with Bennett's cruelty and saved his life even after he abused me," I told her, looking straight ahead, out the windshield.

Felicia placed her hand on my arm, but I kept talking. I needed to get it all out.

"I thought I needed my mom's forgiveness because of my role in the accident that took my sister's life. I thought that because my mom was unwilling to heal, my life would remain suspended as well. It took me two stinging bullets to wake up and extract the right conclusions to this story.

"I've only ever needed to forgive myself. That's all I can truly control."

She nodded but asked, "Then why give Filomena the story? What's the point?"

I shrugged. "To give Bennett the chance to come to the same conclusion I did. It's up to him whether he can forgive himself or not. Maybe he won't realize he needs to, but that's his journey, not mine."

"What version did you give her?"

"One where the shooting at home is included," I said. "Perico's dream was to double tap Jack Bennett." My hand did make the motion as if I were an expert now. "I miss him every day."

Felicia squeezed my arm.

"But he didn't want to understand that bullets can't do the healing." I met Felicia's gaze. "I had to sweep my guilt away before I got too close to you. I think I'm finally there."

Felicia smiled and then bit her lips. "What about Bellatrix?" she asked, looking at me as if everything between us depended on my answer. "Do you have feelings for her?"

"I can't deny that she has a force about her. And she's beautiful, of course. But we're too different. Our journeys don't align. I think, initially, my feelings for her were misplaced. I loved her father. And Perico loved me, but his way of showing it, his version of loyalty, was to try to stop me from saving the life of someone who'd hurt me. Meanwhile, I tried to save Perico from committing another murder."

I laughed. What a pair he and I had made.

"Yet," I said, growing solemn again, "Perico was loyal to me because he hadn't been loyal to his family. I think I represented his opportunity for redemption."

"So, Bellatrix is the continuation of Perico's love?"

I nodded. "I think so. Perico and I were loyal to each other partly because we represented redemption to each other. And I might have shifted this burden onto Bellatrix."

It was the first time I'd opened up to Felicia in this way. Her eyes gleamed with tears.

"I'm sorry for telling you a story that's not pretty."

"I'll take honesty over pretty. You can build on honesty— and loyalty."

Our lips brushed for the first time, and I felt our souls fuse in that delicate caress.

On Sunday, I decided to visit Mom. I didn't want to give her the chance to waver, so I called her on my way.

"Will you go with me to pay a visit to Jenny's grave this time?" she asked.

When I pulled into her driveway, Mom stood by the door, wildflowers in hand. I hadn't smiled at her like that since she had given me a toy plane for Christmas when I was ten. Unprompted, a thought about Filomena receiving the story flashed through my mind. My chest tightened.

This isn't the time to dwell on what-ifs, I told myself. *Be present during this time with Mom.*

I beckoned her to the car, and once she was inside, we hugged for a long time.

"He's your medicine, huh?" she said finally, glancing at Hercules in the back seat.

"I've been on a diet of tears, prayers, and slurps."

The cemetery, bordered by a peaceful forest, wasn't far from the house. Jenny's grave was near the back, closer to the trees. She would have liked that. Dried flowers rested on her stone. Mom handed me the wildflowers.

"Go on."

As I knelt in front of her grave for the first time since the funeral, I could feel Mom observing me, stoic. The sun's rays warmed my face. Without prompting, the words began flowing. For the first time, I felt free to express my emotions about Jenny's death. It had only taken almost dying.

"My Father," I said, bowing my head, "who art in heaven and within me, I bless your name and thank you for this day of reconciliation. Forgive me for not protecting my sister that day as I should have. I pray for healing and restoration. Help my mom and me renew our relationship so that the hurt and sorrow fly away toward you. And through your power, fill us with acceptance for each other, our flaws, and our misguided decisions. Let your light illuminate this new part of our lives. I worship you because you kept me alive when I didn't want to remain in this world."

I lifted my eyes toward Mom. Her expression revealed turmoil, but she nodded at me to continue, then lowered her head.

"My Lord, I take responsibility for my actions. Let us now accept the blessings that will come, and let our joy be complete."

Mom knelt beside me on the warm stone. Soft tears fell from her eyes. I grabbed her hand and looked at Jenny's grave. "My beautiful sister, forgive me. I forgive myself. I'll see you again one day."

My mom and I kissed the stone and each other's hands, and as we lifted our hands to the sky, we sent kisses to heaven.

With that, Hercules stood and dared me to chase him.

"I think he's trying to tell you something," Mom said with a wide smile.

"Maybe he is," I said. And so I let go of his leash and lunged toward him. He took off, making us laugh, and returned at full speed once he'd reached the trees. It felt good to be playful again.

I had prayed with Mom, and progress was at hand, but it felt fragile. I stopped and looked at the trees. She stopped beside me. My heart raced.

"Tell me once more how it happened. I want to see if I can withstand it with peace this time."

"I had just picked her up from her boyfriend's house. She'd broken up with him. I've felt guilty about keeping this secret from you, but she didn't want you to know. She felt you were restraining her from being happy." I turned and took my mom's hands. She squeezed mine.

"The snow came down heavy." I swallowed. "Jenny noticed a giant spider on her arm." I shuddered. "A black widow."

"She hated spiders," Mom said. A tiny smile appeared on her face.

"We'd just passed the barn bridge when it happened. I was driving too fast for the conditions, so when Jenny swatted in my direction, I got distracted and lost control, and we went off the road. The car smashed against the tree. I got her out of the vehicle before the car exploded, but she was already gone."

For a moment, I closed my eyes and breathed heavily until Mom grabbed my hand.

Mom gazed beyond me and gave a slight nod. "Do you understand what happens when a child dies before their time?" she asked without venom. "It does something to a mother. It's not that I haven't wanted you to be happy." She exhaled. "You were responsible for her that day."

Ever since the accident, Mom had said these words. The message hadn't changed. But the tone had. There was no anger this time. Finally, I grasped her intense sorrow; though I had my own, empathy had been impossible until now.

"Yes, I was responsible," I said. It was the first time I hadn't tried to justify my actions.

Then Mom pulled me close and clung to me, and her sobs, my sobs, reverberated within my body. "I forgive you," she said. "And there's something you should know," she continued. "I was also responsible. But not in the way you might think. I don't regret trying to protect her from that boy." She pulled back and looked at me. "You and Jenny always wanted to know why I always wear something blue."

"Yes. Why?" I asked with a frown, surprised by this sudden turn in the conversation.

"I had a difficult pregnancy with her. And when I was in labor, I heard the doctor say to your father, 'Who do you want me to save, your wife or the child?' Your father said, 'Both.' It was typical of him, trying to save everything and everybody." Her eyes softened. "You're like him in that way—much better in every other way. Anyway, somewhat delirious, I promised God that if he saved your sister and me, I'd wear blue, the first color that came to mind, in some form for the rest of my life. The day before the accident, I decided not to do it anymore. I was tired of it, so I rebelled against God. And now I have to live knowing this. I couldn't carry all that weight alone."

Realization dawned. "So you felt guilty and blamed me instead?"

She nodded. "I couldn't carry the burden by myself."

"Why didn't you talk to me?"

"I wanted to. God knows I tried. But the guilt consumed me." She broke down in my arms.

"It's time to leave that behind," I said. "The two of us together, healing at last."

"What are your plans now? Will you get another job?"

"I don't think so, Mom. I've invested too much energy in this one. And I even shed blood," I said wryly.

One thing I knew for certain—I wanted to continue studying with Professor Levine and maybe write a different sort of story.

Second Ending

Chapter 18

ANDREW AND PROFESSOR LEVINE

Tuesday, November 12

I finished the first ending. Perhaps it's time to quit.

Professor Levine's reply to my brief email came at once: *Stop by my office around four to chat.*

I slapped my desk in frustration. Why couldn't he have just said "Andrew, you've worked hard enough, and we can make do with these pages"? I'd left the story, with the first ending complete, outside his office early Monday morning.

Just before 4:00 p.m., I made my way over the uneven brick sidewalk to his building, almost tripping on the roots of one of the old trees that pushed up the bricks until their veins were in plain sight.

The professor waited for me outside with the manuscript held against his chest. Part of me was nervous because his opinion was so important to me, but the other part had complete peace, since I had poured all my being into the page. "Let's go for a walk,

Andrew. There's a place a few blocks away, and the ambiance is suitable for writers."

Professor Levine carried the manuscript close to his heart.

I knew the coffee shop he was referring to and just nodded.

"You're doing it, Andrew," he said, weighing the paper in his hand.

I snorted, and we walked in silence the rest of the way.

The approaching trolley car blared with its powerful horn, startling me. Just two days ago, at Mom's place, the flames had engulfed Jenny's love letters inside the brown mahogany box. The loud waves from the train shook my feet and core, like when I burned the letters. After it had passed, Professor Levine moved nimbly across the tracks.

A couple of blocks later, we reached the shop the professor had in mind. Several students waited for their drinks next to a handful of high-top tables. Chalk of assorted colors declared on a blackboard that the bagels and sandwiches had room for personal tweaking. The barista who greeted us sported a hat made of white cardboard that resembled a coffee cup on a saucer. It was balanced atop a head of frizzy red hair.

"Your usual, Professor?" asked the young man.

"Miguel, give me something different. Make it two. Strong. Really strong."

I couldn't argue with that.

We sat at a table near the back wall so we wouldn't be interrupted. "Miguel here is one of my second-year students," Professor Levine said, smiling at him as he delivered our drinks— cappuccinos with double shots of espresso.

As soon as Miguel was gone, the professor got to the point. "What's this nonsense about quitting?" He took a sip and closed his eyes as he swallowed.

"I haven't been feeling well lately," I said, giving him a grim smile.

"Your eye?"

I nodded and sipped my coffee as well. "It tastes like figs."

"My favorite," he said. Professor Levine leaned back and inhaled the aroma of his coffee. Then he stared at me, and I saw his Adam's apple contract. "We have to figure out a way for you to finish this piece that's not too taxing on you."

"The surgeon said I shouldn't exert myself after the operation." Seeing the professor's look of confusion, I added, "He feels we caught it in time but that it would be best to remove the affected area from the cornea, as the outline is changing, an indication it might be cancerous. Otherwise, it is 'kicking the bucket' time," I said, trying to lighten the mood.

"Please. I wish you would not say that."

"All right. I'll try to be more serious. Anyway, he told me not to look at a screen for a week afterward."

"Does Bellatrix exist?"

I jolted a little at the mention of Bellatrix and the abrupt subject change. "Does she ever, Professor. Does she ever."

Images scurried across my mind, and lying on her bed took center stage. It was obvious to me we had chemistry. Then again, women in her profession were skilled at making men feel comfortable. I didn't know what was real and what was my imagination, and this was only exacerbated by the fact that I'd been out of the dating scene for so long.

"Couldn't she look after you once the operation is complete?"

I laughed at the thought. *A woman like Bellatrix doting on me?*

"She's busy. It would be an enormous sacrifice for her."

"Does Bellatrix actually work at a bordello?"

I sipped my coffee and looked away.

"Right," he said. "No need for me to know." He folded his hands on the table. "I like how you've developed the character of Perico through Bellatrix." He grew thoughtful. "Now, we know a lot about Perico. What we don't know are the motivations behind Bellatrix's actions—that would be beneficial to explore."

As much as I liked the idea of spending more time in the company of such a beautiful, intelligent woman, it gave me pause. I thought of how she'd handled the dagger. "I don't know, Professor. You realize I'd be completely vulnerable."

"Do you trust her with your life?"

"The other option is going back to Greenfield. But that's complicated." The unanswered question hung in the air. The truth is that as much as I liked her, I hadn't interacted with her in multiple situations. Was I willing to find out what she was really like? So I gave Professor Levine the long answer. "Felicia has been wonderful, but I want to protect her from things that are a little complex to explain. I haven't given her a chance yet. That's the truth." I exhaled and rubbed my hands. "And part of me wants to see what happens with Bellatrix."

The professor smiled. "Now the truth is coming out, Andrew. I think Yoyo has some trust issues when it comes to women. Perhaps this is an excellent opportunity for your protagonist to overcome the problem."

I scoffed. "Bellatrix and I aren't even friends, let alone romantically involved. Asking her to care for me while I recuperate? That's a gigantic leap. Don't you think?"

"Call the woman. She might turn you down. But what if she says yes?"

I gave Professor Levine a stern look but couldn't deny he was making some sense. We ordered another round from Miguel, and as we waited, I noticed some young women at the table beside us. One smiled at her friend and turned her notebook around for her to see. Their laughter was contagious.

Maybe I did need to establish a deeper relationship with Bellatrix.

Our drinks arrived.

"The other major issue is Mr. Bennett," Professor Levine said, rubbing his head, bringing my attention back to him. "Bennett, as a character, cannot look at himself and say, 'I did not have a fair chance on the page.' Now, if he rejects the story's purpose . . . That's different. But I think Bellatrix and Bennett are the main characters you need to spend some time with at this latter stage."

"Yes, I remember you saying it was why I needed the second ending."

"Right, and the endings will intertwine in the reader's mind, even though they're separate strands. Both will suggest that Bennett's fate is fair. At least, that's my hope."

"So, you're saying he's doomed, Professor?"

"No, I'm saying that Bennett is the author of his fate. We get what we deserve after we choose our path. That's the beauty of the system."

"Now you're getting philosophical," I said with a chuckle. "I've tried to give the character a fair chance. You know that. And the other one, my life on the page—I don't know. It's rough some days. Healing requires all your strength, physical and spiritual."

It was the first time—well, perhaps not—that I admitted to Professor Levine in an obscure way that the real and the fiction weren't too far apart.

"Look, Andrew, perhaps it's Bennett trying to kill Bennett. And who writes a book to save someone?"

I wanted to tell him everything, my fears, hopes, and how I wanted to free myself from the fetters holding my spirit. But instead, I simply said, "I have difficulty accepting that he's trying to destroy himself. And to your second statement, something good may come out of the spontaneity of the heart."

"Something useful may spring from your exercise of free will. But what I meant about the character is that it has a trajectory. If you let go of a ball from the top of a hill, what could change its descent?" He gave me a fatherly glance over his mug. "Have you stopped to consider that?"

I looked at him, stunned. "My premise is that we still have to try," I said, pounding the tabletop. Coffee spilled over the edge of my mug.

The professor held up his palms. "Hear me out. Mr. Diedra enables him to be cruel, but it's ultimately Bennett's decision. How many murders can you avert?" He pursed his lips and gave me a veiled smile. "I mean, on the page, of course."

"I hate it when you're right, Professor Levine. Free will, huh?"

"Yes, free will. Start writing the second ending. And don't steer Bennett where you want him to go. Let him grab your hand." The professor rubbed his hands and then put both index fingers over his lips for a moment. "You did a decent job with the free will issue in the first ending, when Bennett chose to attack before reading the story, but now, give him another chance on the page. Remember, it's all about Bennett having a fair chance, okay?"

"Okay, I'll let him grab my hand. And you're right. The character chooses, which is important. But I won't let him grab anything else."

That made him laugh so hard that the students beside us turned around and smiled.

"And one more thing, Andrew. Remember that you're writing this second ending for Andrew, not for Bennett. If you were writing it only for Bennett, he would have died in the first ending. You're writing it for your—for Yoyo's healing. And so you can get closer to Bellatrix. Get to work, my friend. From what I've read, she's worth writing that second ending for. And in my opinion, she deserves it. To be completely frank, it should be all about her from now on."

"Why?"

"I felt a genuine connection on the page. And I've been a professor of literature for over forty years. I know a thing or two."

I scratched my head. "Looking beyond the page, huh, Professor?"

He lifted his hands and twisted his lips in true Levine fashion.

"I hope you'll indulge me in one last question. The first ending feels a bit rushed. Is there a reason for that?"

I breathed deeply for a moment to contain my emotions. "I thought I was dying. Ever since I learned about the possibility of cancer being so close to my brain. I didn't know if I could finish writing the story. Yes, I rushed it."

He stood and patted my back like a father does when a son confides something deeply troubling. Choosing him to be my professor had been one of the best decisions of my life.

We walked back to his building without another word. We split, exchanging a shake of hands while looking into each other's eyes with solemnity in front of the redbrick building.

PAGES FOR THE PROFESSOR

Tuesday evening, November 12

In the background, I heard music, chattering, and a woman's laugh when Bellatrix answered my call. I glanced at the river; its surface was smooth and dark blue. Alongside it, despite the cold weather, true to New England's erratic climate patterns, a mother jogged with her baby in a stroller. Her face was flushed, but she seemed determined to keep up her pace. The baby's face was immutable, his perception of his surroundings so different from that of his mother's. Contemplating the river gave me peace. Alongside, on the lagoon, a rower paddled while the lover caressed his leg.

A perfect moment for both.

"Hi, Andrew. What an honor."

"I wanted to call you. There's something I'd like to ask you."

"Where are you now? It sounds like you're outside."

"I'm at the river, near your workplace. By the small lagoon."

"I know the place. I'll be there in ten minutes. I walk fast." Her voice became flirty. "Should I wear something special?"

My heart rate picked up, but I said, "No, come as you are."

"Is everything okay?"

"I suppose so."

"I'll be right over, Andrew."

Leaning against the metal guardrail of a small bridge made of stone, I waited for Bellatrix. The sun had begun its descent. In the light breeze from the east, I caught the scent of the river. A fragrance filled with life and hope.

I'd never seen Bellatrix from a distance. The breeze blew her hair over her face, reminding me of a weeping willow tree. Her steps were long and purposeful, her stride elegant. It captivated me. She smiled while approaching, leaving me speechless.

Her fingers grazed my hand as she turned to look out over the water, as I'd been doing.

"It sounded important."

"It is." I bit my lip to ease my nervousness. It didn't help. "I'm about to have an operation, and I wanted to ask if you'd look after me for a bit afterward. I know it's a leap, since we don't know each other that well."

"Yes," Bellatrix said without hesitation. "I'm already doing it anyway, with a gun and a dagger. I'll put the stiletto next to the pillow before I fetch your milk and sing you a lullaby. And I'll set my .22 next to your grilled cheese sandwich. You'll die when you eat it."

She burst into laughter.

The professor had been right, as usual. For the first time since the attack, I felt like a man, open with the idea that this could involve vulnerability.

Monday, November 25

It had been a week since the operation, and the recovery had gone well, since I spent my time resting. Plus, Bellatrix was dutiful about the medication. The anesthesia had worked fast during the operation, and as I drifted off, my thoughts had been about reconciling with my mom—and about what would ensue for Hercules if anything were to happen to me. I recalled these thoughts as I attempted to write for the first time since surgery. Following the doctor's orders, I used a pad of paper and a pen, no screen.

Over the last few days, I'd met Bellatrix's other side, which contained unparalleled sweetness sprinkled with tactful speech.

"Why don't you dictate," she said, "and I'll write. That way, you're not exerting yourself." Before I could respond, she took the paper and pen away from me. "Better yet, why don't I record our conversation? And then you can transcribe it later. How does it sound?"

I grinned. "It sounds like a great idea." That was perfect. Perico had never held the pen, but perhaps Bellatrix could etch her own thoughts into my story.

"What do you miss most about my father?" she asked formally, as if this were a real interview. Then she smiled. "Sorry, I've always been curious about Dad's life."

"His cursing," I said without cracking a smile. "It was so on point—I mean, honest. Perico was open about his life. He didn't pretend to be a choirboy. And Perico and Hercules, they connected." Then, it was my turn to untangle her mystery, so I asked, "What really happened to you the night you met Freddy?"

She looked surprised, and then her eyes darkened. "After my father went to jail, the state took my sister, and a couple took me into their home. Zemira was lucky—no harm came to her," she said, nodding. "But me? That's another story. My second night there"—she exhaled—"the door creaked open, and then I felt a warm body and a hairy torso on me." She looked toward the window. "Afterward, I fled, and that's when Freddy found me at the bus station."

I tried not to gag because there was more to that last sentence. Her eyes told me she couldn't commit to words the rest of what took place with that man. She glanced at me with a tragic grin.

Her gaze turned icy, but it wasn't directed at me. She grabbed the dagger and squeezed the handle. Sweat accrued on her forehead.

"Bellatrix . . ."

She got up abruptly and stalked to the bathroom across from my bedroom. I heard the water running, and when she returned, the hair around her face was soaked.

"I'm sorry," I said. "I didn't mean to upset you."

"I'm fine. I've never talked to anyone about it, and you've been more than open with me. Let's keep going. Why did you decide to call me before your operation, Andrew? And please don't give me platitudes. I'm accustomed to hearing crap all the time, so I can smell it. I want the truth."

"I was out of options. And . . ." I hesitated, not sure whether I was ready for complete vulnerability, but I went for it. "I wanted to get to know you a little better."

"What about your mother?" she said, ignoring the second part of my answer.

"Mom and I have had a difficult relationship since my little sister's death. There's some reconciliation needed."

"Aren't you afraid of me, knowing what I do?"

"I was a little, at first, but not now. You remind me of Perico, and he'd never hurt me. He'd toss me against the wall, but nothing beyond that. He wouldn't bury me in the wall."

"I'm not my father," she said, almost upset. "I'm colder than him. His violence was mostly related to his job as a bouncer. He navigated a murky world where a job title was avoided. Awful environment! Sometimes, he'd come home with blood on his shirt. One day, he even had a bloody ear in his pocket."

I grimaced. "Really? He never told me about that."

Bellatrix lifted her right hand, meaning she swore it was the truth.

"He said to me, 'I'll return it to the man it belongs to once he gives me the money he owes my boss.'"

"Would you be capable of doing such a thing?"

"C'mon, look at me. I'm a lady." She winked.

I did look at her, and that's when I realized Bellatrix hadn't worn makeup since she'd been at my house. I was suddenly puzzled as to why she wore it in such an elaborate fashion at work. She didn't need any. She was naturally beautiful.

Hercules jumped off the bed and wagged his tail while glancing at the back door, so Bellatrix took him to the backyard. When she returned, I asked, "Why are you loyal to me? What's your motivation here, Bellatrix? I need to know."

Bellatrix smiled. "Simple. You were loyal to my father. I might not have been close to him, but he was my blood. He wanted to protect you. What's weird is that I do, too—and not just out of loyalty."

We looked at each other, knowing we were entering unfamiliar territory. Her hand grazed my fingertips.

"When you came to see me at work," she said, her voice barely more than a whisper, "you didn't come with a slick tongue or try to sell yourself. That made me trust you. There was no deceit in you. You were vulnerable in front of me. After that, I knew I had to protect you." She met my gaze. "I've never fully trusted a man before. All of them wanted something from me, but nobody has ever approached me with purity. Granted, I rent my body for money, but I guard my heart with my life."

"So, why the side gig, Bellatrix?"

"Why not?" she said with a sarcastic laugh. "I provide a service. I'm the trash woman. I dispose of what's rotten. And before I met you, I had never postponed an execution."

I grinned nervously.

"Thank you for that. Tell me more on your thoughts on loyalty. It seems to be a valuable commodity in your life. In that way, you're like your dad, Perico. He always made me pay the price if he even suspected I crossed him in the smallest ways."

"Well, it's complex," Bellatrix replied. "It can be based on anything. For example, you and I were both sexually abused, and that created a bond. We understand each other's pain—the feeling that sticks with you afterward. And you were loyal to Dad, even knowing he might commit a crime. You didn't rat him out. I'm sure there was a profound battle within you. Right? You could have been harmed by remaining loyal to him."

I made a yoyoing motion with my hand and smirked.

"Right. And I gather that Dad expected loyalty from you because you two freely shared the ugly thoughts within your hearts."

I felt tears form.

"I know that my secret about my side gig is safe with you," she continued. "You'd never betray me because loyalty and vulnerability work together. Sometimes, I think about divine loyalty," she said, looking thoughtful. "God never demands it. We have free will. We are free to love, free to hate. Then there's loyalty on the dark side. That one, it's tyrannical. Our beloved Mr. Bennett offered to buy Dad's loyalty. Bennett tried to dominate Dad, not to better his life."

I thought, *How could she know this? Chuchoka. He was always in the middle of everything. It's the only explanation.* "How did you come to all these beliefs, Bellatrix? Surely you didn't get this knowledge reading the Sunday paper." I'd felt all of this in my heart but had never been able to articulate it.

"I'm artful in keeping people away, so I've had time to reflect on what interests me. Besides, when you do my kind of work, you study people who don't think anybody is observing them. It's the best time to do research. Most men assume I don't reason as well as they do because I have a pretty face and rent my body for money."

As fascinated as I was by the conversation, I felt my eyes growing heavy.

"Not so fast, mister." Bellatrix tapped the nightstand, just as she had that day at the bordello.

"Can I write an IOU?" I asked, half-asleep.

"I'll take it."

The IOU was still on my nightstand in the morning but in two pieces. Bellatrix had torn it in half.

Chapter 19

Tuesday, November 26

"I SMELLED BACON IN my dream," Bellatrix said when she walked into my room the next morning, rubbing her eyes. She wore one of my T-shirts and an old pair of my cutoff shorts.

I grinned. "I don't remember smelling anything in my dreams."

"Do you have any bacon?"

"Check the freezer."

I soon smelled the aroma and heard the sizzling. Hercules bolted to the kitchen. Minutes later, a sharp pain shot through my eye, and Bellatrix rushed in to see the reason for my yelp. There was a thumping noise from the kitchen.

"Hercules!" Bellatrix shouted, running around the living room. "Hercules stole the bacon. It was hanging from the plate. I'll kill him."

I laughed again. "Throw another piece into the frying pan. And don't put it too close to the edge of the counter after it's cooked. He's small, but he has a good vertical jump."

When we finally had our bacon, we chewed happily. I couldn't remember the last time I had breakfast in bed. Bellatrix sat on a nearby chair.

"I wonder if they serve this in hell," she said. "No need for a frying pan there. It would probably become crispy on the spot if you threw it on the street."

She continued to surprise me. "I just can't picture you there," I said. "Certain people, yes. But you?"

"Why, because you have feelings for me?"

Her bluntness shocked me into silence. She was right, though that wasn't the only reason I couldn't picture her in hell. I could see her goodness. Before I could tell her this, she laughed and continued.

"I actually do think that one day I'll be there," she said with a shrug. "I eliminate people for a living and sell my body for a piece of paper. Those aren't the attributes they're looking for in heaven."

"If a sinner nailed to a cross repents right before he dies and immediately goes to heaven, what does that tell you?" I said. "People can avert what seems unavoidable. You can repent and change your life."

She looked away and focused on her bacon.

Hercules sat waiting for scraps and put his paws on Bellatrix's knee, and his tongue flew from side to side. His desire for bacon was more potent than his fear of the woman who'd chased him through the house.

She gave him one scrap from her plate and took one from mine to give to him as well.

"I sometimes imagine it," she said. "I see this expanse with everything ablaze, even the guard's little house. The sizzling metal bar that holds in the tormented goes up when the provisions from heaven arrive. They have to last for thirty days. The water comes in glass jars. But it's so hot that when I drink, it burns my throat. My skin melts away. Bennett is there." She glances at me. "He lives in a special chamber reserved for tyrants. It's a hole in the ground with an even higher temperature. He walks with a dagger stuck in his chest, and the blood around the wound is dark. He can't take the dagger out because the metal handle is red-hot. The blade and the flesh have become one. His pain is constant."

I could feel the murderous part of Bellatrix in a way I'd never experienced with Perico. I felt the weight she carried. But all I said was "You have a strange imagination, Bellatrix."

"Right now is the time to have one of those." She shrugged again. "Because, once you're there, it's pointless. Don't you think I examine my life every night? Sometimes even while a man deposits his essence into me." She shook her head. "He wants to preserve what he knows is fading—so he puts it into a prostitute. Isn't that strange and pointless?"

She laughed, but her mood had become so somber that Hercules put his paws back on her knees, perceiving her gloomy attitude, and licked her hand, though this time not for the bacon.

"Why torture yourself like that?" I asked.

"Who knows? Maybe it will end up changing my life for the better. Right now, I'm in a labyrinth, and I can't see the way out."

"Professor Levine would love to have you in his class."

"Why?"

"Because he enjoys discussing the philosophy of life and death. He knows a lot about life, but you're the expert in the other one."

"You're right. But me, taking a class? That's the funniest thing I've ever heard."

"Funnier than Bennett trying to get to heaven?"

"Do you think Bennett is trying to get to heaven?"

"No, but I'm writing this story so he doesn't go to hell."

"Like I said, you're a romantic," she said, shaking her head. "I like numbers, Andrew. Facts. What are the chances he reads the story and then changes his behavior? It won't happen."

"I believe he'll at least consider it. A man whose life was saved twice—shouldn't he take a second look at how he lives it? And if he doesn't, that's on him. His fate is fair because he made it."

"But that's the thing, he's never seen the loaded weapon reserved for him."

I remained quiet. She was right.

That night, she tapped the nightstand again.

"I'll write another IOU, okay?" I said, with my eyes half-closed.

Wednesday, November 27

The following morning, the IOU was once again torn in two.

Bellatrix was observing me.

"How long have you been watching me?" I asked groggily.

"I've been thinking," she said. "You want to save a man like Bennett, to forgive him, and yet you've still not reconciled with your mother? That's not cool, Andrew. Let's drive to Greenfield this weekend. Or would you not be proud to introduce me to your mother?"

I was fully awake now. Reconciling with Mom at Bellatrix's suggestion?

"Are you prepared?" she said.

"I warn you. My mom can be difficult. I was there not too long ago, and we made progress, but—"

"Oh, I see. You forget who you're talking to. I read people on the spot and react accordingly. Do you trust me, Andrew?"

"Of course I do. It's not a matter of trust. I don't want to put you in an uncomfortable situation."

"It's nice of you to want to protect me, but I take care of myself. Haven't I proved that to you? Not that I have to prove anything to you."

I nodded. "I'd certainly be proud to introduce you. But meeting the family? Are we at that point?" I hadn't even been able to acknowledge I had feelings for her. But the situation and the moment—my whole body and heart—answered the question without delay.

"Who knows? I know I want to go with you." Her body language didn't contradict her words. "Anyway, this is more about you than me. Tell her we're friends. She'll make her own assumptions. When was the last time you brought a woman home? You see my point."

"I do."

———

Bellatrix suggested we walk across the street to Ryan Park to watch the sunrise. My convalescence had kept us in the house for days. As we walked out the door, Felicia returned to her house wearing jogging clothes.

Without hesitation, she crossed the street and hugged me while greeting Bellatrix. Felicia looked as beautiful as ever, but there was sadness in her smile.

"I've been missing Hercules," she said.

"You can walk him anytime," I said. "He misses you, too. He's always parked near the door, waiting."

Bellatrix observed us with a cautious expression on her face. My heart tightened for a moment.

After saying our goodbyes, Bellatrix and I made our way to the park. As we approached a sandy area housing a swing set, my steps became heavy, so we sat down on the swings. On the other side of a chain-link fence, there was a basketball court, and farther down was a baseball field.

I closed my eyes and exhaled, and when I opened them, I instinctively held my breath. A skunk wiggled our way, bold and pretentious. It looked at us with fierce, shiny eyes. But its tail didn't go up. I took Bellatrix's hand but remained still otherwise, as if dead.

We were at his mercy, and we knew it. What caught my attention were Bellatrix's eyes. I'd never seen them look so powerless.

Finally, the creature ambled away.

This time, we both exhaled.

"I have a suggestion, Andrew. Why don't you give Bennett the story as it is right now? First ending, that's all. There's enough there for him to get the message."

My heart rate picked up. "And how do you suggest I get it to him?"

I'd told Bellatrix what Professor Levine had said about the second ending, that it was more for me than anything. Healing was happening, and Bellatrix's care had made an enormous difference. My confidence was up, yet I was about to confront the beast. The thought aroused plain old fear.

"Call him and say there's something you want him to read. Maybe tell him he owes you because of what he did to you. Up to you."

"But I already talked to Filomena with the hope she'd give it to him."

"You can still give it to Filomena and have her be a beta reader. A variation from the original plan is okay."

I was rattled, but she looked so sure about this. Her eyes had an intensity I had not seen before, so I drew strength from her. "I don't know if this will work, Bellatrix."

"It will work," she said. "But when you tell Bennett that he owes you, don't make it sound threatening." She looked directly at me. "I'm not a person who's in the business of providing opportunities. A threat is an opportunity. It can backfire on you. So, unless you're prepared to be more like me and walk through the door with a gun or a knife—don't threaten. There's nothing worse than a person who threatens but doesn't deliver."

Her words had weight and authority, and she convinced me. Bellatrix took away my fears for a minute, long enough for me to agree to do as she suggested.

"Where do you think the handoff should happen?" I asked, realizing that Bellatrix deserved a say. She'd been a huge part of all of this.

"Not your place, that's for sure," she said in her low tonality. "Public spot. Give Bennett a copy of the manuscript and see what he does. That's what we've been working toward all this time, right?"

"I thought I was giving the story to his daughter," I said. It was my final attempt to change her mind. "It felt safer."

She made a dismissive gesture with her hand. "I'm a direct person, Andrew. This way, you ensure he has the story. Isn't that the whole reason you're writing it? So he can read it? We can't force him, but if he doesn't, that's on him."

"Yes, but still . . ." Perhaps I'd been secretly hoping Filomena wouldn't show it to her father. Or that Bennett wouldn't know with certainty that I'd been writing about him. "I might bring things with Bennett to a showdown this way."

"And what were you expecting?" she said with a scoff. "This isn't the moment to be indecisive or weak. Didn't you say my father called you Yoyo because you went back and forth in your opinions? He was right about you," Bellatrix said, with an unfamiliar coldness in her tone. "You're a yo-yo when it comes to your emotions."

Her words hurt more than when Perico lifted me off the couch and tossed me back. I got off the swing and walked away a few steps.

"There's a lot at play," I said, turning back.

"Yes, Andrew, you're right. A life is at stake. Whose? I don't know anymore."

I turned, and her eyes pierced me. "Call Bennett," she said, speaking with the power of one accustomed to doing business involving terminal consequences. I'd grown so used to seeing the softer side of her that the reminder of her lethality jarred me.

"Have you thought about what you'll do if he doesn't change?"

"Yes," she said. "Sit down, Andrew, and I'll describe it to you." She patted the swing next to her.

I was tense, running my fingers over my head.

"We've established that you're a romantic. Real life is different. It's not one of the imaginary worlds you've constructed. You need to build these worlds to remain sane. I didn't build one after that beast raped me. Instead, I took care of him. No second chances."

"You mean . . . ?"

She looked beyond me. "I did what I had to. I treat people like they treat me. And I charge even more to take out the garbage than I do for pleasure."

I stood again, uncomfortable with the direction the conversation had taken. If life was anything, it was a stream of chances. I wanted to tell her this. But I remained quiet. She'd stung me.

"Sit down, Andrew Joseph. We'll compare how far from my imagination Mr. Bennett's actual fate is. Jump in anytime. But better yet," she said, with her bare feet floating above the sand, "you try it, Andrew. Come on. Improvise. You need to do this for your healing."

I was taken off guard. She'd gone from encouraging to frustrated.

She was so much more than the fantasy woman who played a role at the bordello or the dark professional bringing lives to a halt. She was a woman with profound thoughts—and a knot in her heart.

"Okay," I said, clearing my throat. "Here I go. Ready?"

"Yes, give it to him," Bellatrix said. "Stand up straight."

"Bennett shows up at the restaurant in the market near the ocean. The manuscript rests on the tabletop.

"'What's that?' Bennett asks.

"'A story I've written,' I say. 'You're one of the main characters in it.'

"He smirks. 'I'm probably the hero.'

"'On hell's clipboard, perhaps. And with no remorse.'

"'Remorse is a weakness.'

"The waitress brings the menus, and without looking at her, I say, 'We need more time.'

"Bennett continues. 'You don't realize, Andrew, that my boss gave me the go-ahead to treat you as I choose because of Mrs. Mejia's case.' He eyes me. 'Yes, that's right. I have his backing. What do you have? Who's supporting you? You're all alone. I can do as I please with you, and nobody can stop me. Before, you had Perico, and look what happened. Did he help you?'"

Bellatrix's eyes steamed with anger, and her body tensed. The veins in the forehead and neck came to life. But she said, "You're doing fine. Go on."

"'Read it and see if you're so protected,' I say, slamming my hand on the manuscript. 'Call me after you read it.'

"Bennett grabs the manuscript with his left hand and extends his right to caress my hand. I take it away fast and spit on the floor beside his shoe.

"'I think you liked it too much the last time,' he says. 'And this must be a love letter—a long love letter.'

"'I know why you're so bold in your evil, Bennett. Because you think, including your boss, that nobody can tell the story—because we don't believe extreme wickedness is possible until it smacks us in the face. Right?'"

Bellatrix held up a hand to stop me and searched my face. "Even you don't think he's changed." She ran her thumbnail across her throat with blazing speed. "That's my message," she said. "Do you feel Bennett had Mr. Diedra's full backing in what happened to you?"

I nodded.

I reflected on her words, which had sliced the morning air. My worst fears for Bennett seemed an undeniable reality.

"That's as far as I can go today with this fantasy, Bellatrix."

She reached for my hand, which I'd laid over my throat.

"I'm proud of you. You took the second step today. The first was writing about what he did. I know I said earlier, Why write the second ending? But the more I think about it, I agree with your professor. Finish the second ending. That's your job now."

I sat down on the swing.

"Few victims confront their abusers," she continued. "People like Bennett count on that." She got so close to my face that I felt her breath. "Do you still think he's worth saving?" she whispered. "Say the word, my love. I crave to hear you say it. And I'll make it as painful as you want me to."

I dropped to my knees in the sand, holding my head. But she dropped down, too. I felt tormented, like with Perico's machinations to help me in his tortuous, sick way, which had never stopped. But she wasn't finished.

"I felt a connection with you, Andrew," she said, sounding more vulnerable now. "I have since the night I met you. I don't know why. It goes beyond my father. This whole thing is new to me. In my world, people aren't saved. They're only used and discarded. Killing is in my blood. I mean, your desire to save someone—I've never experienced that. Maybe you came into my life to teach me about your world. I might reject it. I don't want to mislead you. But I know I at least have to consider it. This, helping you, might be the closest I'll get to your form of healing."

The chilly wind engulfed us and entangled the strands of our hair. Bellatrix leaned her head against mine. It had been easier to discuss feelings with Perico. What I felt now was something I hadn't experienced in a long time. Perhaps never. It complicated everything. I didn't know how to oppose her murderous desires without creating a precipice between us. And right now, near the end of the narrative, I needed her to be on my side.

"Look at me, Andrew," she said, and I raised my chin to meet her gaze. "Once you give the manuscript to Bennett, anything can happen. But remember this: No matter what happens, you've won. You've fought back, and the best part is that he won't have expected you to do this, to defeat him with subtlety, with a story—with forgiveness. That's the Master's touch."

"Why can't you find your own form of healing, Bellatrix?"

She lowered her head.

Back in the house, the lights stayed off. The sheers glowed with nascent light. In my bedroom, I inhaled Bellatrix's lilac scent while she ran her fingers over my face and neck. I closed my eyes. Her lips embraced me, and I tasted her fire.

Chapter 20

PAGES FOR THE PROFESSOR

Friday, November 29

WHILE BELLATRIX WAS STILL in my bed, I sat on the couch with Hercules by my feet. I heard the traffic on River Street and the Mattapan trolley blaring in the distance. I'd dreaded this moment since I began writing the story, though I hadn't expected it to play out like this.

It was eight o'clock when I dialed his number and set things in motion. My body froze when I heard Bennett's voice. My mind returned to the moment he zipped up his pants while singing that dreaded song whose lyrics I dared not reproduce, as I'm convinced they'd come from hell.

"Hello? Hello?"

"Hi. Mr. Bennett . . . I . . . I have something for you, a story I want you to read, but I won't be at work until Monday."

"Why wait? Give it to me today." I heard the smirk in his voice.

"Very well. I haven't been out of the house much since the operation."

"I can come to your place if you prefer," Bennett said. His tone was forceful.

"No, I don't think so," I said in an equally strong manner. "Public place. What about near the Park Street subway entrance at noon today?"

"I'll be there," he said.

When I ended the call, Bellatrix stood beside the piano, caressing her hair and wearing only a long T-shirt.

"So today is the day?"

"Yes." I ran my fingers through my hair and cleared my throat, hoping to appear confident before her. But she read my moods without a problem.

"Until now, writing the story was a romantic dream of how to fight evil. But the moment Bennett takes the manuscript, whether he lives or dies is on him."

"Will you come with me?"

"Of course. But I'll wear a disguise. We have to maintain our advantage." She curled her body against mine.

"Romantic dream?" I said, kissing the top of her head. "Is that how you view what I'm doing?"

She lifted her head to meet my gaze. "Yes, but there's nothing wrong with that. And if you follow through, the romantic becomes tangible. You haven't just contemplated Bennett's wickedness, but responded. That's a romantic action grounded in the real world."

My breathing became labored, and Bellatrix held me tight

as I cried tears of release. The story had traveled through a web of opposition.

I kissed Hercules before we left, and we walked to Mattapan Square. We took the inbound trolley to Fields Corner station. The car wiggled like a skunk, and I gripped the metal bar in front of me. Bellatrix wrapped her arms around me.

"It'll be okay, Andrew," she whispered near my ear. "I'll be there with you."

When we reached the station, I called Mom to tell her I was coming home the next day and that perhaps it was time to go to the cemetery. It was time to be decisive and grounded in the real world.

"I'll have company," I said at the end of the voice message.

From Fields Corner, we took the inbound train to Boston, and twenty minutes later, we walked up the long stairs leading to the street at Park Street station. Bellatrix wore dark glasses and a scarf over her hair. People buzzed in and out of the converging Red and Green Line trains. The smell of pee was faint, but I noticed it right away. I walked ahead, knowing Bellatrix trailed not far behind. I stopped at a park bench while the leaves swirled around my feet.

"Andrew. You have something for me?"

I whirled around, startled.

His voice elicited a wrenching sensation in my solar plexus, just as it had ever since the attack.

Without a word, I held out the manuscript. My heart raced.

Bennett looked at it and laughed. "This will take a while to read."

I only shrugged, then turned and left. My knees felt weak, but I kept walking. If the man only knew I'd averted his murder twice.

When I returned to the station, Bellatrix grabbed my hand and squeezed it. Relief washed over me. It was done.

Back at home, I settled in my desk chair, and Bellatrix sprawled on the bed beside me. I lifted the shades for the first time since the attack. It felt as if I'd given Bennett the story a long time ago.

"What goes through your mind when you do your job—jobs?" I asked. "I'm not trying to pry. I just want to understand you better. You are still a mystery."

"Do you want to know?"

I nodded. "It's part of who you are."

"I think I probably can write it better than saying it out loud. If I write it, there's a distance. You're not looking at me. Do you understand? Perhaps I'm not making sense."

I smiled. "I understand better than anyone."

She grinned. "May I sit in your chair?"

I stood and offered her the seat. "Write a few paragraphs. They could become part of my story with your permission, so you have a voice in this whole affair. The second ending, you know?"

Bellatrix turned to my computer and started typing. "*I always wore makeup when I was with a man*," she said, reading her words aloud but waving me out.

"Hercules, it's time to go to the park," I said with a particular urgency.

It would be my first walk alone since the operation. As Hercules and I strolled, I imagined Bellatrix walking into my childhood home. I pictured all three of us going to the cemetery. It was such a short time since I'd met her, but there was no one else I felt such a bond with.

Hercules and I lingered at the park. I was eager to read Bellatrix's words but didn't want to interrupt her flow.

When I returned, Bellatrix was on the bed looking at the ceiling. "It's a glimpse into an escort's mind," she said, gesturing to the computer.

"Why don't you read it aloud?"

And so she did.

"I always wore makeup when I was with a man. Stupid, I know—childish even—my intention, I mean. But it was my way of protecting my heart. I envisioned the makeup as a shield between his flesh and mine, my heart and his. It's a shield, a shield, *I thought in my chamber that first night, trembling. The old woman came in, rubbed my teeth with vodka, and said, 'It'll help.' But I coughed, so she stopped. She sucked her teeth and slammed the door on her way out. 'You'll learn to listen to me,' she said from outside the door.*

"The first time I used makeup, I told Freddy I wanted to earn a living. I was a tall, skinny young woman whose breasts budded at winter's dawn. The low tonality of my voice helped. My

need for independence outweighed my scruples. With the makeup, I wanted to make myself more beautiful to break down the man before me. I wanted him to be powerless. Yet taking off my clothes petrified me. And when one of them demanded the extras, I closed my eyes.

"I knew I was supposed to moan after they made noises. I counted to twenty before unleashing the serenade I'd practiced in the mirror. 'Give them a good show,' the old woman had said. That first night, while showering afterward, I stayed under the water for half an hour, stopping only because she screamed, 'Don't use all the hot water! It's only a little sour milk between your legs.' I cried and hoped the water would cover my sobs. The man's smell was still in my nostrils when I went to bed. So, I got up and brushed my gums raw until I saw blood swirling on the white porcelain and into the drain.

"Every time, I put the powder on my face, and then, at the end of my ritual, I'd use my middle finger to place a dab in the valley between my breasts to protect my heart. Last night, with Andrew, I didn't wear any makeup. It's the first time I'd ever done that."

Bellatrix stopped and met my gaze. I didn't move a muscle, not wanting her to stop. The moment felt sacred. I wanted to hear all her thoughts, even though it would take time to process them.

She continued. *"I feel that what Andrew does, constructing imaginary worlds, drafting this story to save a man like Bennett, doesn't differ much from what I do—putting powder between my breasts. It's all in my mind that the makeup will protect me. I want to heal from that beast that raped me as a girl, and I don't know how. Perhaps Andrew's onto something. I mean, writing about his situation—about the coward who attacked him from behind."*

I swallowed, and my eyes flooded. But I made Professor Levine's circular motion with my hand.

"I knew it would be painful when my fingers struck the keyboard. But more specifically, maybe I'm afraid to heal. I wonder if I'll lose my powers. That's what bothers me. What will happen if, by a miracle, I heal? I'd have to change my whole life—the only life I've ever known.

"Huff!

"I'm puzzled by Andrew's reluctance to judge me. He's curious but doesn't pass judgment.

"And about the other gig, I believe transforming a living being into a corpse replenishes my sense of power. Looking into their helpless eyes, begging me like when I pleaded with that hairy beast. There were eleven steps from my pretend mom's door to my room."

Anguish filled me.

"I don't show them any mercy. And when I see their legs wet, I tell them, 'Sorry, baby, your pain is my gain.' But in the end, we're all powerless. My power, anybody's, is all an illusion.

"But let me get down to the ground again. I use makeup. Some women use drugs. If you think Andrew is deranged, think about the men who choose to lie with a woman on drugs at the place with the red door. These men are living a fantasy, depositing their semen into someone they don't know, who'll treat their essence worse than trash. We're all living a fantasy just to make it to the time when the night comes to overpower us, and sleep becomes our drug."

Hercules seemed to be trying to decide which one of us to comfort. It didn't take him long to jump into Bellatrix's lap. He put both paws on her chest and slurped her pale cheeks until she hugged him.

"Are you sure you want to take me home to meet your mom?"

I was certain.

That night, we slept over the covers with our clothes still on, tangled up together.

I woke up only once and signed the IOU for her. This time, she hadn't asked me to.

Chapter 21

Saturday, November 30

STEAM ESCAPED INTO the hallway as I pushed open the door, and the water from the shower drummed in my ears. I slid the curtain and told Bellatrix I'd load the car. Her sweet eyelids flickered, and I contemplated the water trickling between her narrow valleys and the mole on her cheek. I wanted her to stay forever.

Back in the bedroom, I noticed the handle of the .22 peeking out of her purse. A gun was not a new sight for me as of late, but I always felt troubled because only a speck of time separated the slumber from the roar.

As I put my foot in the sneaker, my toes met with resistance. I picked up the shoe and found several pieces of torn paper—last night's IOU. I grinned. Her creativity seeped into our little mementos. I put the pieces in the clean spaghetti sauce jar with the others. I wasn't sure why, but I felt the need to preserve them.

When I returned to the house after loading the vehicle, Bellatrix walked into the living room, ready to go. Her hair was split into two braids. She wore jeans with one of my white button-up shirts and a dark tank top underneath. As for the makeup, she had only a touch of lip gloss. I enjoyed this peaceful look of hers. She didn't need all that golden glitter around her eyes.

"How do I look?" she asked, twirling for me.

I embraced her and let my lips glide off hers, barely touching. I felt a twinge in my heart, a little pressure that let me know something had budded. Her eyes told me she knew exactly what was happening.

She ran her fingers through my hair.

"There's something else we should do before we leave to see your mom," she said. "Let's take the version of the story you gave to Bennett to Filomena."

"Why?" I asked, confused.

"Because this way ensures that he'll get the point. Even if he discards it, she won't let it go without questioning him. A double tap."

I texted Filomena. *I have the story ready for you.*

She replied, providing me with an address on Massachusetts Avenue. And after printing another copy of the story, Bellatrix and I headed out the door.

"I haven't been on a road trip in a long time," Bellatrix said, climbing into my hatchback. Hercules had decided to walk beside her as if they were old buddies. When she was settled, he climbed on her lap and stuck his head out the window to bark at any passing dog. Bellatrix held the manuscript on her lap as well. "Are you nervous?"

"A little. Mom and I have been stubborn in holding on to our pain. So I'm glad you pointed out the obvious."

She nodded. "You've gone far on this healing journey. Why leave a stone unturned?"

"I don't know about the sleeping arrangements," I said, glancing at her. "I hope you're cool with whatever happens there."

"I don't worry about those things," she said, resting her hand over mine on the console after setting Hercules on the back seat.

I took Jamaicaway to Boston and headed for Massachusetts Avenue. We stopped near the school's entrance on Boylston Street, where Filomena and her friend waited for me, resting their backs on the redbrick wall. She looked happy and relaxed.

I felt a twinge of guilt and hoped the story wouldn't upset her too much.

Bellatrix and I got out of the car, and I greeted Filomena with a wave.

"Here's the story," I said, handing her the manuscript. "Let's see what you think."

"Your girlfriend?" Filomena asked, smiling at Bellatrix.

Bellatrix circled her arm around my hip and smirked. "He wishes."

When Bellatrix didn't offer anything else, Filomena focused her attention on me again. "Do you have other beta readers?"

"Your father, actually."

She frowned. "Dad?"

"I mentioned I'd written something," I said, trying to sound relaxed. "And he agreed to read it."

"Huh, well, maybe that's good. I'll compare notes with him."

"Here's the thing," I said. "I'd prefer you didn't, so there's no interference. I'm interested in unbiased responses."

She nodded. "Okay."

"Send me a text when you're done. No rush, Filomena. Take as long as you need."

We waved from the car, and I exhaled, taking a moment to compose myself before beginning the next leg of the trip to Greenfield. Hercules already had his head out the window again, behind Bellatrix.

"Was that deceptive of me?" I asked Bellatrix.

"Borderline." She frowned and added, "She'll figure it out anyway. The hidden always makes its way to the surface. Stories have a way of making that happen, don't they?"

I didn't answer. My mind raced into different scenarios, like me getting hurt, which was what Mom feared. I turned up the heat since it was getting cold outside.

We headed north on the interstate in bumper-to-bumper traffic and over the Zakim Bridge. An hour later, we were in New Hampshire. And a half hour after that, we began ascending the mountain up to Greenfield. Water from recent rains flowed over the rocks next to the road and traveled to a small aqueduct, passing underneath the road to the river basin.

About ten miles from Mom's house, we made a pit stop for Hercules, but when it was time for us to take off again, the engine wouldn't turn. After several attempts to start the car, I was forced to call a towing company. Thankfully, Bellatrix didn't look worried at all. Her calm demeanor put me at ease.

The flatbed arrived in twenty minutes, and after the vehicle was loaded, Bellatrix, Hercules, and I settled next to the driver, Pete. I felt him glance my way a couple of times.

"You're from Greenfield, right?" he said finally. "Have we met?"

He had a long beard and a greasy shirt. Nothing about him was familiar to me. "I don't think so," I said.

"I remember now," Pete said. "It was a long time ago. I saw you at the scene of an accident. By the covered bridge. Your car burned and I ended up towing it."

I tensed up. I wanted to get out of his truck. Bellatrix sensed it right away and took my hand.

"I was in shock," I mumbled and shifted my body away from him. I didn't bother telling Pete that my memories of the time right after the accident were blurry. Only the most upsetting images came through.

"Do you come back regularly to Greenfield, buddy?"

"Not at all."

Bellatrix squeezed my hand again tighter. In fact, I had visited once several years ago, but my feet refused to walk across that bridge. I'd turned around and returned to Boston without stopping to visit Mom, even though I'd driven by the house.

The ten-mile ride seemed to last forever. When we arrived, Pete unloaded the vehicle in my mom's driveway and promised to return with a new battery in the morning. Hearing the commotion, Mom came outside and stood by the door.

Bellatrix approached her right away, and Mom welcomed her with a smile and an embrace. Hercules lifted his leg right next to the doorpost.

"Not there, Hercules," I said.

Mom knelt and petted him.

The house looked better than the last time, and the grass had been mowed. Bellatrix and I looked at the maple floor and took our shoes off. At the top of the stairs, in the sunroom, Bellatrix pointed to Jenny's painting. In the kitchen, there was one of Jenny with Mom. Both were painted by Jenny.

"It's good to see you again, son. You made my dream come true by bringing a gorgeous woman home," Mom said.

"Thank you," Bellatrix said, kissing her on the cheek.

"Why don't you rest for a while, and then we'll eat? You can use your old bedroom. And Bellatrix can use Jenny's."

Bellatrix embraced Mom again and thanked her for the gesture.

I led Bellatrix upstairs and laid our shared suitcase on a chair in Jenny's room. Hercules scoured every room before joining us. It felt as if Jenny might walk through the door at any moment. Everything was in order. There were no spiderwebs or dust, like the last time I visited Mom, and the air smelled fresh. All her perfume bottles stood perfectly aligned on the dresser, and when I opened the drawer, her clothes were still there. I removed a shirt and smelled it.

"That's strange," I said to Bellatrix. "It's warm like it's just come out of the dryer."

She frowned. "No, it can't be."

"Touch it."

I lay on the bed and rested my head on the pillow. Bellatrix commented on how beautiful the room was, but I couldn't keep my eyes open, exhausted from the tumultuous emotions of the last days. Hercules twirled on the spread next to my legs, and when I opened my eyes again, Bellatrix sat by Jenny's bazaar, as I used to call it, with the large mirror. The frame was all mahogany. I remembered carrying it to her room after Mom bought it for her. We almost fell, carrying it up the stairs.

"I'm going downstairs to spend some time with your mom, Andrew. I'll tell her you don't feel well so she won't get upset."

"Tell her I just need a quick nap," I said. By the time Bellatrix returned, the room had gotten dark.

"Andrew, you need to go to your room," Bellatrix said next to my ear, waking me. "We shouldn't offend your mom. You, too, Hercules."

"How long were you downstairs?" I asked groggily.

"A couple of hours. Your mom showed me pictures of you and Jenny. You were a cute baby. She cried, too," she said softly.

"Did you eat?"

"We had salmon, brussels sprouts, mashed potatoes, and your favorite dessert—lemon pie. Don't worry," she said with a grin, "I left you smelling like fresh lilacs. I also told her about the operation and the great care I provided."

I stood and was about to leave when she said, "Aren't you forgetting something?"

She handed me a small piece of paper and a pen. I scribbled my initials, and after kissing her, I left.

Resting on my old bed felt strange. It was smaller than I remembered. My old typewriter was on the desk. Mom had sanitized the room since my last visit, which was good because she was taking control of her house; after all, I didn't live here anymore.

At first light, I heard a knock. Bellatrix marched in and threw herself on the bed. "We have a busy day today. The guy's changing the battery in the car right now. I gave him the keys. What do you want to do first?"

"I want to go to the bridge where Jenny died. It's about four miles from here." A couple of days ago, when my mind had been dealing with giving the story to Filomena and Bennett, I'd decided that going to the bridge where the accident had happened was the first order of business.

"Do you want me to go with you?"

"Of course."

Downstairs, breakfast was ready. We said our good mornings as we settled at the table. The butter dish, a white cow with a hairline crack, stared at me. A couple of days before the accident, Jenny had broken it in half with her fork. Mom fought with Jenny about her boyfriend. "A womanizer like your dad," Mom had said. My sister knew Mom relished that cow because it was an antique.

I couldn't believe Mom had kept it.

Bellatrix broke the silence. "We're going to the covered bridge between Bennington and Greenfield. Would you like to come?"

Mom shook her head and shoved a bite of scrambled eggs into her mouth. I chewed my toast.

"I'll go to the cemetery," Mom said a few moments later. "But not to the bridge. I usually drive far out of the way to avoid it." She stood and went to the window, her eyes fixed on the forest behind the house.

I got up, walked to her, and put my head on her shoulder. It was a start, a new relationship between us.

Bellatrix and I drove down Forest Road, where the old town hall stood royal, all white and majestic, on a grassy hill. Soon, the houses became fewer, and the trees got thicker. After crossing Old Bennington Road, I knew we weren't too far from the bridge with its brownish walls. Bellatrix didn't say a word, though I felt her glancing in my direction. My heart pounded so fast that I had to pull over. I got out of the car, and Bellatrix knelt beside me on the side of the road. Spit hung from my mouth like a spiderweb glued to my lips.

We walked the rest of the way. The dry road was covered in fallen leaves, and the gravel crunched under my weight. A car approached. It clunked and rattled as it crossed the wooden and metal structure. I kept my gaze where the crash had occurred.

I walked until I emerged on the other side of the bridge. Hercules and Bellatrix trailed me.

"I thought I'd never return to this place after the last time I was here," I said, breathing heavily.

"But you're here."

There weren't any marks on the ground, and the river flowed with ease. No signs of the tragedy that had occurred. I pointed at the spot where the car had been. Wordlessly, Bellatrix wrapped her white scarf around a nearby branch. Right away, it fluttered as if waving at us.

I hugged Bellatrix tightly and allowed tears to come.

"There was a major storm that morning," I said, with my face near Bellatrix's ear. "She called me and asked for a ride home from her boyfriend's house. I told Jenny to stay put until the storm passed."

"Why didn't she stay?" Bellatrix asked softly.

"Mom heard the conversation and demanded I pick her up at once. She hated Jenny's boyfriend, and Jenny had never spent a night out."

"You had no choice."

"We always have a choice."

"Talk to your sister now, my love. Tell her about your desire to heal."

I knelt again and looked up at the scarf.

"The guilt is like a heavy coat, Jenny. I've convinced myself I deserved all the misfortune. But I've come here to free myself from that awful energy. Every day, I carry the weight of your death, and I can no longer do that. It's destroying me. Today, I release that weight to the universe. From now on, I will live a new life in your honor." My voice cracked. "And I will always love you."

I stood, and we crossed the bridge again. Vapor rose from the reedy water in the early morning light. There was total peace. I held Bellatrix tight against my hip. Hercules watered any strange smell he encountered.

Back in the car, Bellatrix held me for a long time. I let the peace continue to wash over me.

"What now?" she asked finally, pulling away. "We have to make this trip count, my love."

"I suppose we could take Mom to the cemetery after lunch, but . . ." As I spoke the words, I realized I was still angry with my mom.

"What's the problem?"

"Her way of dealing with all of this has been to ascribe all blame to me."

"That woman is in pain, Andrew. She misses her daughter. Be empathetic. Even if things don't go smoothly today, listen to her. When Jenny died, a part of your mom died. Why do you think she washes and dries her clothes daily?"

I scoffed. "I have no idea."

Her eyes flashed. "She must, or the pain will kill her. She's doing what she needs to do to survive. She hasn't fully accepted Jenny's death and tells herself daily that her daughter is coming home that night." Her tone grew firm. "Be a man. When you're a man, you protect, even when it's difficult. I know you're a man, despite what you may believe because of what happened to you."

I blinked in astonishment.

"Just spend some time with her. Show her love. Why do you think she's still alive? For herself? No, for *you*. She knows her role. She's a mother. Now, be her protector. If she wants to pound on your chest, let her unleash her fury on you. I'll respect you for it."

I nodded, but she continued.

"You know the stuff I wrote for your story? I put on makeup. Your mom warms your sister's clothes in the dryer. It's her fantasy."

It made so much sense in Bellatrix's voice.

"I can perceive so much pain in that house. It travels all the way down the stairs from that tidy room on the second floor. Jenny's soul is crying to be set free. She needs our help."

"Then let's help Mom to free Jenny and herself."

The door was unlocked, so we let ourselves in. Hercules beelined for his food bowl. Mom had prepared lunch, and there were flowers on the table.

"I hope you like them," Mom said to Bellatrix. "They're for you."

Bellatrix kissed her cheek. "Thank you. They're beautiful, and the smell—petunias, right?"

"Yes. I wanted to give you something beautiful, like you."

The first course was soup. "I made it with pumpkin and added some cream," Mom said. "It gives the house a pleasant scent. Fried trout with salad is the second course. Now, tell me about how you two first met."

"Through an associate of mine," Bellatrix said.

"I noticed all my old clothes are gone." Mom didn't say a word. Bellatrix gave me an intense stare. I cleared my throat. "You probably donated them to somebody who needed them more."

"Yes, dear," she said with a peaceful look.

"Thank you for letting me stay in your daughter's old room," Bellatrix said. "It's very comfortable."

She smiled sadly. "'Jenny's bazaar,' as Andrew calls it, was Jenny's way of feeling special in her room. I hope it did the same for you."

Bellatrix nodded.

I debated whether to ask about the warm clothes, but, as though reading my thoughts on my face, Bellatrix gave me a soft kick under the table.

"Delicious meal, Mom."

The encounter wasn't going as I'd imagined. Bellatrix's presence had changed the dynamics. My last visit smoothed things between us.

"Any dessert?"

"Yes, blueberries and cream. I thought it might bring back some memories."

I couldn't help but laugh.

The three of us walked to the cemetery despite the absence of a sidewalk, thinking the walk might help us prepare for the moment. The graveyard was before Zephyr Lake, which provided a breathtaking distraction when going out of town.

Mom looked fragile. We had to hold her as we approached the granite stone. Bellatrix tried to hand Mom the flowers.

"Will you put them in the vase for me?" Mom asked. She'd frozen at the sight of the sepulchre.

"Yes, of course." Bellatrix kneeled and placed them in the old greenish glass vase on the tombstone.

I helped Mom kneel and then got to my knees beside her. Her lips moved, but I couldn't hear the prayer. After a minute, she looked up at Bellatrix. "My dear, would you say some words? I feel Andrew and I aren't up to it."

I was grateful for Mom's request. The bridge visit had sapped my strength.

Bellatrix nodded and bowed her head. "Dear Jenny, we're here to pay our respects and speak with you in the hope you can hear our voices. We wanted to come here sooner as a family, but our pain didn't allow us," she said, as if she had been part of our nucleus for a long time.

"Through Andrew, I've seen glimpses of who you were—your passions, your playfulness, and your hopes. When I'm gone, I'd like to know that just one person loved me as you've been loved all these years.

"Your mother's heart aches for you. In this brief time, I've perceived her pain. But the love she has for you is greater than her sorrow. And I'm confident Andrew will love you even after his death because I've seen his loyalty to you in life.

"You're irreplaceable. Yet we, the living, need to heal from this tremendous loss. We must move on now. The love we have for you will never change, though. Never. We love you, Jenny. We'll see each other soon."

Hercules snored on the grass and twitched as if he was having a dream.

Over Mom's shoulder, I caught Bellatrix's eye and mouthed, "Thank you." She knew me even better than I'd thought.

On the drive home, I thought about the week ahead. I was supposed to show up at work the next day, and Bellatrix was going back to her job. Both made me feel restless.

"I'd consider making some changes in my life," Bellatrix said, unprompted, looking at me from the passenger seat. "Maybe move to Greenfield with a green-eyed man. But only if he has a dog, though—the kind that steals bacon from your plate. You know, live a quiet life."

Stunned, I glanced at her. I wouldn't get my hopes up just yet, but a man could fantasize.

"I need to think about it some more," she continued. "But why not? I have more than enough saved for a time like this." She kissed her fingers and put them on my lips. The sunlight ricocheted off the lake. "This seems like a good place to heal the soul's wounds."

Back in Mattapan, Hercules ran inside ahead of us and checked every room with quick and decisive steps. Bellatrix and I laughed. "He's trying to take my job away," she said. Then she grabbed my hand and led me to the bedroom.

Shortly before midnight, she ran her fingers over my head to wake me up, then tapped the nightstand. I turned on the light, scribbled the three letters on a purple pad, and turned off the light again.

Chapter 22

Monday, December 2

BELLATRIX'S RASPY WHISPERS TO Hercules enthralled me as the sound of her voice traveled from the kitchen. The momentary silence filled me with anticipation for another word. When I opened my eyes in the bedroom, the torn purple paper with the IOU wasn't on the nightstand beside the lamp as usual.

I sat up on the edge of the bed and placed my feet on the cold wooden floor. Today was the day. I took off the clothes I'd slept in and showered in a rush.

In the kitchen, Bellatrix leaned against the counter, drinking a fresh brew. Steam rose from the cup she'd prepared for me. Her blue jeans and dark parka hugged her body, and she'd pulled her hair into a ponytail. Her lilac-scented perfume took me to a patch of wildflowers on the park trail.

"Are you prepared for what's coming?" she asked when I walked into the kitchen.

I shrugged and took a sip. "I'll have to be." But a new uneasiness traveled through my core.

Hercules was restless but had already eaten. I considered asking about the IOU but decided against it, not wanting to spoil our intimate communication. I headed back to the bedroom. Next to my wallet and keys was Bellatrix's perfume. It was the first time she'd left it there. I grabbed it and thought about asking if she'd forgotten it. But nothing Bellatrix did was accidental, so I left it where it was.

"You got all your stuff?" she asked while her eyes examined my every movement and expression.

"I got everything. And you?"

"Yes, I have all my things. Don't forget what's happened here between us."

"It's impossible to forget those eyes," I said, moving closer to her.

"I've allowed nobody else to get this close to me. You know what I mean?" she asked, playing with my shirt buttons.

I was about to kiss her when my phone rang. Looking at the screen, I groaned. "Oh no, Chuchoka again."

"Answer it," she said.

Reluctantly, I did.

"You forgot about me?" he said by way of greeting.

I held the phone near Bellatrix's ear.

"Never, Chuchoka. What can I do for you?" I said, frowning but with a steady tone.

"Do you know why I'm calling you?"

"Let me guess—Bennett, your life's obsession. I gave him the story over the weekend."

"You did?"

"Yes, so it's up to him now."

"And Bellatrix, what about her?"

She nodded and whispered, "She knows everything."

There was silence on the line for a moment. "Is she there with you?" Chuchoka blurted before I could relay her message.

"Why do you want to know?"

He snickered like he had that night when he nicked my throat. "You lucky bastard. You have the lip and can talk your way out of a paper bag."

"You'll never understand, and it has nothing to do with luck."

"Are you coming back to work soon?"

"I'll be there this morning."

"Let's have lunch on the roof," he said.

"Do I have a choice?"

After hanging up, I felt pressure in my chest. Bellatrix seemed to sense my discomfort. "We knew he'd be in play at the end. He's a meddler."

"Yeah, it's true, but he disgusts me," I said and shook my head several times. "And you're right, he has a small role to play."

In the car, we didn't say much. During a moment alone at the house, Mom had asked me how serious things were between Bellatrix and me. "Serious enough," I'd said. But now, what was on my mind wasn't Chuchoka or Bennett or his reaction to the story, but that Bellatrix would be working at the bordello.

It's her job, I told myself, trying to focus on what she'd said about making changes. I knew this wasn't trivial.

Bellatrix glanced at me and read my mind. "Andrew, we're figuring things out between us, right?"

"Yes."

"So don't overthink it. Concentrate on dealing with Bennett and Chuchoka. Our stuff will work itself out." She grabbed my hand and squeezed it tight. "You chose a woman who has some baggage and a complicated life. This is new for me."

"Thank you for taking care of me," I said in a subdued voice. I didn't want her to go.

The wind sent wave after wave of reddish leaves blowing over the car's hood while I drove the curved road. To my left, a woman rode her bicycle uphill on a path covered by leaves. The water in the pond next to her was choppy. She balanced her body over the pedals and rocked from side to side to advance. Moving just a few feet required all her strength. To my right, the glassy buildings were observant and immutable.

"Drop me at the next light," Bellatrix said. "Send me a message this evening."

She gave me a quick kiss and crossed the street. I contemplated her walking away, engulfed in swirling leaves, until an insolent horn reminded me of the green light.

The Charles River awaited the megaphone to break its slumber, while my feet advanced robotically toward the middle-aged gray building and the stench of garbage by its rear entrance. The green dumpster provided the rats with a hefty gourmet breakfast. My presence didn't rattle them. I locked eyes with their ringleader, and the slimy bastard stared back with a fierce, shiny gaze. He shrieked and fought for stale pizza crust. I was a stranger in his territory.

My heart rate increased as I entered the building and pressed the black button to call the elevator. When I emerged in the basement, I found Chuchoka leaning against the wall outside Bennett's dark office. He snickered a pitiful salutation.

"Bennett is out," he said, narrowing his eyes at me. "The boss said Bennett took the week off at the last minute. Some sort of emergency."

My gut churned. The story. He'd read it.

Chuchoka continued. "Strange for Bennett to take time off like this."

That morning, strolling at low speed behind my buffer gave me anguish for the first time. My stomach growled, adding to my unease. Bennett was capable of violence. The hallway lights seemed overly bright, and I wanted to escape to the roof. When lunchtime arrived, I ran up the metal staircase.

Whenever the weather got colder, the door to the roof stuck in its rusty frame, so I kicked it hard to let out my frustrations. Chuchoka sat contemplating the river by the stony ledge and turned when he heard the thumping. Silence reigned for a few moments. Being here with this madman felt irreverent. This was Perico's spot. Suddenly he got up.

"Should I be worried that you're getting too close to the Specialist?" Chuchoka finally said. He paced back and forth.

"I don't think it's your business." It felt strange hearing him call Bellatrix that. I now knew her as a sensitive woman with complicated professions.

"It's very much my business. Your closeness with her might affect her judgment."

"Something tells me that getting close to her won't affect the outcome you're looking for. After all, you want Bennett dead, don't you?"

"It doesn't feel right for Bennett not to show up at work," he said, ignoring my comment. "And you said you gave him the story? Coincidence? I don't think so."

"Why don't you call him if you're so worried about him."

He glared at me. "I did. You look like you're doing better. If something were to happen to the boss, it wouldn't affect you anymore, would it?"

"Are you trying to get out of your promise to Perico?" I snapped, tired of restraining his murderous desires. "Never mind. What you do is your business. But Bellatrix and I agreed to let Bennett read the story and take it from there. Let's see what he does. Don't forget, you sent me there to avert the imminent."

"Right," he said, frowning. "But did you consider how he'd perceive the content? Before, Filomena was going to tell him about the story. That was your hope, right?" He paused. "I wonder what Perico would have thought about all these extra opportunities for such a man?"

I snorted and glanced at Perico's shriveled tomato plants. "He would have called me a yo-yo for sure."

"I'll keep close tabs on him, but I suggest you lock your door at night," Chuchoka said with a hint of concern. Did he care? "Do you still have Perico's .38?"

"I do. But let Bennett decide what happens to Bennett, okay? Otherwise, what's the point of having waited all this time?" Before heading back inside I asked, "Do you think Bennett will do something stupid?"

Chuchoka nodded. "I'd keep the gun under your pillow if I were you."

"You know I'm not a violent man."

"Under the right circumstances, anybody can become violent. Besides, it's self-preservation."

It was the first time Chuchoka had gotten profound.

The evening light drifted away as I approached my house after work. Hercules barked when he saw me coming up the steps, and once inside, I kissed him as if we hadn't seen each other for weeks.

When my phone rang in my pocket, I assumed it was Bellatrix. She'd texted earlier to ask me to pick her up on Beacon Street at nine o'clock.

But Filomena sobbed on the other end of the line.

"I finished the story. Why the hell did you want me to read it? And don't give me any shit about needing a beta reader."

My silence indicted me. I had to drag the words from my mouth with a chain. "Where are you? This is a conversation we should have in person."

"I'm outside the library. You better tell me the truth, Andrew, or I'll never speak to you again."

"I'll be there in half an hour."

I showered, changed my clothes, and was out the door again in ten minutes. Hercules couldn't believe I was leaving, so I bribed him with a toy I'd hidden for a special occasion like this one.

Jamaicaway was dangerous at night. Nothing but a double yellow line separated the cars on the winding road. Still, I flew down it.

Filomena sat on the steps leading up to the library. Her eyes were locked on the large granite stones I walked over.

I reached out to touch her shoulder, but she pulled away.

"Don't. Don't! What were you thinking, Andrew?"

"I wasn't trying to hurt you. I didn't think it through. At least not this part of it, how you're taking it."

"How I'm taking it? How else would I have taken it? I had a huge fight with Daddy today. I'm not sure I ever want to see him again."

My heart ached for her. That hadn't been my intention. "He's still your father."

She slapped me. My right cheek burned.

"My father is a monster. Do you know what that feels like?"

I hung my head. "No, I don't." I heard my words; the truth was that I knew what it felt like but not from her perspective, from the daughter's side.

She sank to the steps and looked exhausted. "You used me, Andrew, or whatever you want to call yourself. You didn't need a beta reader. You wanted to get to Dad. Why didn't you give it to him and leave me out of it?"

"My motivation was to get him to change. I wrote it to save him from what he'd done. When I started writing the story, I hadn't envisioned giving him the manuscript directly."

She looked at me. "He truly hurt you?"

I covered my eyes with both hands and nodded.

"How can I ever look at him again and pretend everything is normal? I have a father who hurts people."

"Did he say anything?"

"He cursed your name and threw a vase against the wall."

Fear shot through me. Maybe my plan had backfired, and I should sleep with the gun under my pillow.

"I asked him if he'd done anything like this before."

"And?"

"He was quiet for a long time, and then said, 'How can you think that about your father?' I told him he was a coward."

I sat next to her. "Ever since the attack, I've been living in hell, trying to figure out what to do. My thoughts tormented me, Filomena. The possibility of hurting you never even entered my mind."

"It would be easier if I didn't believe you," she said, sniffling. "I don't know if I can go home tonight."

"If you don't feel safe, call me."

"Give me a few days, and I'll send you some feedback if you still want it."

"Of course." I didn't know what else to say.

We hugged and agreed to meet again. But as I walked away over the rectangular granite stones, I remembered the day I ripped my favorite pants tumbling over a jagged rock while trying to retrieve Mom's pearls from behind a rosebush. They had been a gift from my father.

It was impossible to stitch them back together.

Chapter 23

Monday, December 2

DOWNCAST AND DISORIENTED AFTER my conversation with Filomena, I found myself in the dark parking lot beside my car, not knowing how I'd gotten there. A car backfired on Storrow Drive, and the high walls edging the road amplified the sound, making it sound like a cannon going off. It startled me out of my stupor.

I drove to Beacon Street and walked toward the massive red door. It looked different tonight, as if somebody had repainted it with a brighter shade of red, ready to smear whoever entered.

I rang the bell, and a woman in a short purple tunic opened the door. She wore brown Roman sandals, tied up her calf, and carried a toy golden sword.

"She's changing," she said, giving me a voluptuous smile after I handed her the Specialist's card, and led me to the stairs. Soft music played in the background. I took in my surroundings. My first time here, the bacchanalian atmosphere had overwhelmed me. My eyes searched for the plump man. He had either reconciled with his better half or lay in a ditch with a smile.

Just before heading upstairs, I stopped short at the sight of familiar cropped hair and massive arms. The man turned and we locked eyes. Chuchoka lifted a glass of champagne in my direction.

Why was he here? Keeping an eye out for Bennett?

I approached Bellatrix's door with mixed emotions, pleased to be spending the rest of the evening with her, but— why keep thinking about it? I told myself.

She was still in the bathroom when I entered.

"There's something in the drawer," she called out. "Open it. It's for you. I'll be out in a few."

In the drawer, a package the size of my fist rested between the .22 and the dagger. On the package, Bellatrix had signed my name in red. The wrapping paper was deep purple and held together with a golden sash, which I put around my wrist. I unwrapped the package to find a torn purple note. She'd sprinkled perfume on it. My heart sprinted.

There was also another note, intact: *I won't demand payment from you anymore. I know it took me a little time to arrive at this decision. And I never explained why I demanded the IOUs. But I knew you understood. Besides, a woman doesn't want to be rushed. Yours, Bellatrix Sanchez.* I placed the note in my wallet and lay on the bed, savoring the moment.

She looked excited and expectant when she came out of
the bathroom. "You got the torn IOU?" I'd never heard her so
giddy.

I sat up and grinned, tapping my left pocket to show
where I'd placed the pieces of it.

"And the note?"

"It's right here inside my wallet," I said, holding it up.

Bellatrix's hair hung freely over her breasts. She wore a
white silk blouse and jeans. And there was no makeup on her—
not even lip gloss. The lilac scent and bright red nails were her
only adornments.

I walked toward her, holding the wallet over my heart.

"Let's go out and celebrate," she said. Her raspy voice tan-
goed in my ear, and she nipped my earlobe with her playful teeth.

She grabbed her jacket from a chair and opened the
drawer. She contemplated the gun before placing the dagger's
scabbard into her right boot, her usual way of carrying it. But
then, she looked at me and put it back into the drawer. She
locked it and put the key inside her pocket.

"Are you sure you don't want to take the gun?"

"Yeah, tonight is about fun. You'll take care of me."

I grinned. "A new beginning?"

We strolled out of the room, just as Jack Bennett appeared
from the purple door. He examined us for a moment with a
shocked expression. "Are you two together?" he asked, with anger
in his slurred words. His shirt hung unbuttoned outside his pants.

Before either of us could react, he stormed back into
the room and returned with a revolver, a .38 with a mahogany

handle, just like Perico's. A woman wrapped in a white towel followed him and tried to appease him, but he only got angrier.

"My daughter hates me because of you, green-eyed, yoyoing bastard!" He opened the barrel and closed it right back. Then he struck the cylinder. And for a moment, the sound took me back to that darkened room on the fourth floor in Murderpan. Everything came to a standstill, yet my brain computed multiple scenarios at an astonishing speed. In one of them, Bellatrix and I ended up in a pool of blood. In another, I disarmed him and put a bullet in his brain, perhaps two. A glorious double tap.

Aware of Bellatrix standing next to me, I moved her out of the line of fire with an outstretched arm, then placed myself in front of her. Her gun was in the room, locked in the nightstand drawer.

I heard her boots clicking on the floor.

Bennett screamed, "Don't move!"

The sound stopped.

Out of the corner of my eye, I saw movement. Chuchoka slithered up the stairs, weapon drawn. The dagger, a replica of the one he'd entrusted me with, kissed his leg. His back hugged the curved wall leading to the second floor.

Bennett swung the revolver in all directions to keep everybody at bay.

I took a step forward and spoke with an even tone. "You don't have to threaten anybody else. I'm here. Do what you want, like you always do."

I heard a commotion downstairs and sirens in the distance. Chuchoka took two steps toward Bennett. I leaned toward the weapon. Bennett's trembling hand fired a shot. The sound ricocheted off the lofty ceilings. A peal of thunder. Then came a second.

I looked down and my shirt was clean. I instinctively turned.

Bellatrix looked stunned. Part of her white blouse was bright red.

Panicked, Bennett tossed the gun in my direction. I grabbed Bellatrix before she crumpled to the floor. Her blood was on my hands.

The gun called me by name. Bellatrix saw me wrestling with the idea.

"Don't let my life be meaningless," she whispered. "If you kill him, your enemy has triumphed."

I put my hand over her wound to stop the gurgling blood.

"Be loyal to yourself, Andrew, and to me. Because if you kill Bennett, you'll end up dead inside."

I heard a woman's voice coming from the first floor: "Upstairs, upstairs!" Then I saw from the corner of my eye a police officer with his firearm drawn.

Perico's words came to me from the grave: *You're responsible for Bennett's next victim.* Fury engulfed me. "Bennett has hurt too many people, Bellatrix."

"Show me your loyalty by walking away," she said weakly. "Bennett's end will come, but don't let it be through your hand, my love."

She exhaled once more, and a line of blood trickled out of her mouth.

I went for the weapon.

"Don't," the officer barked, stopping me. "You've done nothing wrong—yet." I looked at Bennett; his leg was wet. A yellowish puddle had formed around his naked foot. Gunpowder and ammonia, like two tyrants, overpowered Bellatrix's lilac scent.

I looked back at Bellatrix's lifeless body. I could hear Perico: *You're a traitor if you don't empty the gun on Bennett.*

But Bennett's inferno would trap me forever if I followed my raw instinct. The malevolent seed with which he'd impregnated me would sprout into a life of perdition. I dropped to my knees and let the gun remain on the floor, honoring the dying request of the woman I'd fallen in love with.

The cavernous ceilings amplified the sound of Bennett's laughter.

"You're a punk," he said.

A second later, Chuchoka's blade penetrated Bennett's left lung. My attacker's eyes looked as if they wanted to fly from their sockets. He gasped for air and then collapsed in a pool of blood and piss.

The police officer grabbed Chuchoka, pushed him to the floor face down, and cuffed him. I went back to Bellatrix and cradled her lifeless body. I put my bloody hand in my pocket, and there they were, the pieces of paper now smudged with red.

I had my second ending, but not the one I would have chosen to write.

Chapter 21

ANDREW AND PROFESSOR LEVINE

Saturday, December 7

THE SKY WAS STILL dark when I sent Professor Levine the email. Afterward, as I sat on the back porch, the steps were frigid, and the trees looked like an amorphous collection of shadows. Despite the icy air, Hercules wanted to stay outside with me after he'd run to his naked rosebush, which I'd wrapped in sackcloth because of the winter snow. He gave the once beautiful red petals lying on the ground an untimely watering, and they refused to be resuscitated.

My constant companion snuggled up against my hip. The porch light sputtered out, and darkness overpowered us. Far away in the sky, though, was a timid glow. As time ticked on, the formless bore shape and the blotches of darkness became defined patches of knitted bark.

The unforeseen happened, I'd written. *I finished the second ending but at an abysmal price.*

The professor responded right away. He kept odd hours, and I knew because of the time stamp of his emails. Lately, I had been, too.

Come over and bring the story. I'll be in the office in an hour.

It didn't feel right to leave Hercules behind this time. I'd never taken him to the university, but it was Saturday. Before leaving, I grabbed the printed manuscript and looked at the jar with the notes. How would he understand my pain without them? They were the evidence of my torn heart—the proof that she was real and her transformation. I grabbed the jar as well.

We climbed into the car. Hercules spun before settling in the passenger seat. Curled up, he looked like a snail, and I rested my hand on his dark, shiny coat, which felt like pure velvet.

Jamaicaway offered me glimpses of vapor rising from still water and naked trees with fat trunks. The curves came at me faster and faster, taking me to Professor Levine's office in record time. There was no real rush, but the quicker I went, the slower things became in my mind.

The professor and I arrived at the same time. He lifted his lunch box, and I raised my satchel with the manuscript. We bore smiles thinner than the first insinuation of light on the horizon. Hercules wagged his tail in greeting and sniffed a path to Professor Levine's office.

We walked up the marble stairs in perfect silence, and I placed the manuscript on his desk. Hercules toured the room and then rested against the farthest wall, close to the heating register, after spinning again.

I sat on the floor, leaning against the wall as well, while the professor scanned the pages. With every passing moment, the walls changed tonality almost imperceptibly. The lone sound was Professor Levine's fingers sliding over page after page. Occasionally he'd glance at me, his gaze as serious as I'd ever seen it.

Sometime later, my stomach growled, competing with the swish of the turning pages.

"Let's take a break," the professor said. He removed some cookies from his lunch box and opened his thermos.

Hercules crunched one of the treats I'd packed for him and went back to sleep. The professor and I ate in silence. I was sure he could see my distress. Minutes later, he sat back in his swivel chair and continued reading.

I took Hercules for a walk outside, and when I returned ten minutes later, Professor Levine looked at me for a long time, rubbing his chin with the back of his hand. His face looked ghastly. The bags below his swollen eyes fused with his collapsed cheeks, which was his usual look.

"Did she die in real life?"

I nodded and picked up the jar from the floor. "It's all I have left of her," I said, setting the jar on his desk. "The purple ones, the ones smudged with blood, were the last ones she gave me."

The professor shifted back in horror. Then he put down the manuscript, removed his glasses, and wiped his eyes. "Now I see what you meant by 'abysmal.'"

For a moment, the only sound was Hercules cleaning his coat with his tireless tongue. He'd returned to his spot by the register. Professor Levine examined his rimless glasses, contemplating them in total bewilderment. "Are you up to discussing this today?"

"Yes. I have to, otherwise—" I had to make sense of writing this story and the despair that had followed. And talking with him became therapeutic. "What do you think about how the story ended?"

He looked at me, and his demeanor shifted. He became the professor I knew once again. "I find it interesting that the last scene takes place at the bordello. They are places where pleasure occurs, yet I think they are the saddest places on earth. Some end up trapping the women, and amid the moaning and pretending, the selfishness comes through like that megaphone shouting over the Charles River's silent waters."

I appreciated the imagery. "You're right. The stage for the last chapter had to be able to withstand the misery."

"That nameless man who walked those eleven steps in the darkness trapped Bellatrix in those walls," Professor Levine said. "He loaded the weapon that Bennett fired."

"So, the question looms," I said, standing. "What do you think, Professor Levine? Was Bennett's fate fair?"

"Without a third ending, Mr. Andrew Joseph, alias Yoyo, we'll never know."

"Oh, come on, Professor," I said, exhausted. "Don't do that, please."

"Okay, okay," he said, holding up his hands in surrender. "I'm glad Bennett didn't die by Andrew's hand. And Chuchoka was born to kill Bennett. They deserved each other."

I chuckled grimly. "I'd say so."

"Now I have a question for you, my friend. Why didn't you leave? You could have gotten another job. Gone to a different school. There are many teachers."

"It's true. But I didn't want to run anymore. I'll tell you a story. One day, a while back, when I first moved into my place, I walked home from the supermarket, when three teenagers robbed me. One put his hands around my arms from behind to immobilize me, another put a gun to my stomach, and the third young man put his hands in my pocket. I'd worked hard stripping floors that day, and the idea of turning over my money to them infuriated me."

"In Murderpan?" the professor asked, his expression sympathetic.

"Yes. In a fraction of a second, I made a decision. I rid myself of the guy holding me and punched the guy with the gun. It went off, and then the teenagers ran. Thankfully, there was no blood. It was a miracle. But then I chose to fight a second time—I chased the shooter. He was the oldest of the group. He turned and fired a second time, and I ducked and kissed the asphalt. And then came the crucial moment. I got up while the kid was still pointing his gun at me. Ten or eleven feet away. His eyes spoke: 'I don't want to kill you, but I will if you force me to.' So, I stood still and let him go." I laughed. "I wouldn't be talking to you if I had gone after him again.

"You see," I continued, "there's a time to fight and a time to run or stand still and let death pass you by. It was my time to fight regardless of the consequences. That day with the three teenagers, I learned that you shouldn't fight if you're not prepared to die."

The professor blew out a breath. "You were prepared to die, metaphorically and physically?"

I nodded. "Besides, there's only one professor who believes in me the way you do."

He grabbed the manuscript and wrote on it with a red pen.

"Hercules. Let's go home," I said.

I shook the professor's hand and took my story. Only once I was in my car did I look at the grade. I broke down. I'd put my whole being on the line. It was a miracle that I hadn't died. I lifted the manuscript to heaven as an offering to Him.

It didn't belong to me anymore. It was God's.

Epilogue

There were swift changes at work after Bennett's corrupt doings came to light through a police report that informed the university. The top people in my department were all replaced, but at my level, things stayed the same.

When the weather got warmer, Mrs. Mejia and I started eating together on the roof, but we didn't speak. Instead, we contemplated the river. The place became our chapel; we meditated while the wind and sun bathed us. She even began growing tomatoes on the rubber roof. She filled old plastic containers with dirt and nurtured the seeds, throwing a smile at me once in a while.

Every so often, Felicia still took Hercules for a stroll. He'd jump straight up when she arrived. She didn't leave chocolates on the counter anymore, but she'd started putting bandannas around Hercules's neck, which he seemed to enjoy.

I missed the chocolates and what they meant.

Mom decided to get new kitchen cabinets and also removed the old tub upstairs. The modern shower with a glass door was "very in," according to Mom. Once a month, we had dinner on Sunday, and afterward, we walked to the cemetery.

We'd buried Bellatrix next to Jenny. About a year after Bellatrix's passing, though, Mom said, "I'm not going to the cemetery anymore."

I nodded. It was time. We were sitting together at the kitchen table, which overlooked the rear deck, now painted a light gray, and the railings had a white accent.

Then she gave me one of her looks, from which there was no escape. "What did Bellatrix really do for work?"

I sensed she already knew. There was no room for fidgeting. "She worked as an escort," I said, choosing a word that might sound more palatable to my mom.

She sipped her cinnamon tea. "I knew the moment I saw her," she said with no condemnation. "I saw her hips move and observed your eyes." She grabbed my hand. "Did you love her?"

My chest got tight, and I nodded.

"I knew that, too. So, who was I to tell you to stay away from her? I'd already tried that with Jenny."

I still showed Professor Levine my stories from time to time, and every so often, I read "Lealtad." Whenever I came to the part Bellatrix wrote, I put the story back in its drawer, feeling as if I were intruding on her intimate thoughts. Shortly after my conversation with Mom, though, I read Bellatrix's words again.

The next day, on the roof, I gave Mrs. Mejia a copy of the manuscript and asked her to give me feedback. Specifically, I wanted to know her thoughts on whether I should let people read it, given how personal it was.

"Let people read it," she said, when she returned the story several days later. "They need to know what some women go through and how to cleanse themselves." She hugged me and then held my face in a motherly fashion. "Sometimes, another person reading about our pain is the only justice we'll experience."

After many more Sundays with Mom, she finally revealed the truth about Dad. Whenever I'd asked her about it in the past, she'd just tell me he left and then she'd change the subject. In reality, he had "committed an error with her." Her terminology. And so she had told him to leave and erased him from our lives. He'd sent postcards every Christmas, but I hadn't known. She handed me a stack of them wrapped with an elastic band.

Jenny had an intuition that Mom had driven Dad away, because of a dream she'd had. "Jenny never told you because she knew it would hurt you. She confronted me, and we decided to keep it from you. I'm not proud of it," Mom said, breaking down. "That's why we had such a complicated relationship."

I just breathed deeply. I wasn't angry at her anymore about hiding things. What was the point? It was time for healing. I took the revelations as a sign that a new chapter in my life was about to begin. I decided to travel to the Southern Hemisphere to search for my father. Graduation was around the corner.

I also gave Mom's number to Mrs. Mejia. They both needed a friend.

Two weeks before my trip, Hercules had an accident, and I found him dead when I came home from work. Before burying him in the backyard under the shade of the pine trees, I caressed his velvety dark coat for the last time, with Mom by my side. I opened the sandy ground with a shovel and lowered his body, wrapped in a white sheet. We looked at him in his burial attire, and Mom looked at me. "Speak to him."

"Hercules, if I wrote a book to tell you what your shiny eyes, filled with purity, meant to me, it would not be enough. I never told you this, but some days when I didn't want to go on after the rape, those glistening eyes made me want to come home and fight one more day for both of us. Your eyes stopped a murder when the bullets wanted my blessing in Perico's apartment."

My heart ripped as I shoveled the dirt on top of Hercules.

Hercules's death hit Felicia hard. I went to her house to deliver the news in person and remembered the first day I knocked on that door. We spent the afternoon sharing tearful embraces and memories of how he jumped as if aided by a spring when she was about to put the leash on him. The next day I gave her the story to read. At last, I felt comfortable about Felicia knowing everything about me. "It's all in there," I said, "what we never had the chance to talk about. It has two endings."

Her gorgeous eyes widened. And that miniature dimple on her bottom lip—it took my breath away every time.

"I'm honored you want to share it with me," she said.

I gave her the blue collar Hercules wore on his last day on this earth. "I thought you might want to keep it." We embraced, and I turned to leave. But then I turned back. "I would have liked—"

But she got closer and put her index finger over my lips. "No regrets," she said. "And what's meant to be will be."

I had done my best to save a man's life and failed. But the story had saved me and Mom. I'd thought we were beyond redemption. A miracle of sorts. In a strange way, I think Bellatrix would have approved of the story's result.

Professor Levine had been right when he'd said that the second ending should be about Bellatrix.

Her life had not been wasted.

The voiceless had, at last, shouted from the dark rubber rooftop as if aided by a megaphone over the murky Charles River.

Acknowledgments

I want to thank Rachel Small, my editor, for her brilliant work on *Lealtad*, my first novel. I also wish to extend my gratitude to Ester Vera Ramos for her spiritual guidance throughout this project. Josie Norton also played an invaluable role as my beta reader.

Sarah Lahay created the magnificent art covers and typesetting. Jennie Cohen provided the line editing, and Elyse Lyon did the proofreading. I also want to express my appreciation to Robert Levine, my beloved professor, who saw me as a writer before I realized it was my call.

Now, I must honor my father, Humberto San Martin, who taught me about loyalty, and my mother, Ema Zambrano, who moved me to forgive myself and others, even after her death, through the memories we shared in this ephemeral life.

9 798999 204170 5